THE HENCHMANS
AT HOME

THE HENCHMANS

Thomas Y. Crowell Company, New York

AT HOME

By Hester Burton

Illustrated by Victor G. Ambrus

DESIGNED BY JOAN MAESTRO

Manufactured in the United States of America
L.C. Card 78-171003
ISBN 0-690-37706-1

1   2   3   4   5   6   7   8   9   10

To A. W–H. and her friend N. C.

whose childhood memories of life in a small Suffolk
town in the 1890's have provided the background
to the following, wholly fictitious events.

Contents

The Day that Went Terribly Wrong

≽ 1 ≼

On that golden July morning, Rob Henchman sat astride the garden wall, feeling as proud as a king. It was his birthday, and everything was as perfect as it could possibly be, for his mother and William and Ellen had given him the toy theater, after all; and his father had bought him the knife out of Hindley's shop window. A proper man's knife with two heavy blades and a long, strong spike. He rode the wall with his right hand inside his jacket pocket, clutching it to make sure it was safe, his pride swelling anew as he fingered the back of the blades—for with such a grown-up present, it was clear to everyone that he was out of the nursery forever. His father, at last—at long last—had recognized him as a *boy*. He felt so burstingly pleased at this that he wanted to

ring a bell, like the Rushby town crier, and bawl out to everyone walking past in the Market Place below:

"Hi, everybody! It's my birthday. And I've got a great knife."

But his mother did not like him shouting. She did not even like him sitting on the wall. Besides, his father and William had a great contempt for boys who boasted about their possessions.

Down below him in the garden, the white damask table-cloth suddenly flapped into the air like a swan taking wing.

"Hold on tight, Florrie," cried Cook, "or you'll have it caught in the rosebush."

Florrie giggled and held tight.

Rob liked Florrie's giggle; it made him feel happier still.

Now they were spreading the cloth over the trestle table and patting down the creases, making little clucking noises as they bustled about. This made him happy, too. For it was *his* party they were so busy with. Not Ellen's or William's.

2

But his alone. He had chosen the guests and the jellies and the games. And last week—without telling anyone—he had dashed across the Market Place and invited Mr. Brooks, the draper, to come to show them his conjuring tricks. He had done it on his own. It was *his* day. Not William's. William would not even be there. He was away at boarding school. Rob gripped the warm bricks between his knees and shut his eyes in pure bliss. For the first time in his life, he—Robert Henchman—would be absolute lord of his own party.

Then, suddenly deciding that this day of days should be remembered for ever, he opened his eyes again, took out his knife, unclasped the long, strong spike, chose a particularly clean and splendid brick on top of the wall, and carved:

JULY 10th, 1891.

Then, just in case posterity should think that this was some-one else's day—and not his—he added with a flourish:

R. H.

"What are you doing?" shot Ellen sharply from three feet below his left foot. She was standing on the edge of the narrow flower bed, peering up.

"Nothing much," he replied warily, not liking to be caught carving his own initials.

But the "nothing much" betrayed him. A puff of brick dust blew off the wall into Ellen's upturned face.

"Yes, you are," she said accusingly, wiping the dust off her cheek. "You're ruining your new knife. You'll 've turned the blade, you silly."

"I'm not silly," he replied hotly. "I'm using the spike."

"Well, don't lose your temper. And come down from the wall. Mother doesn't like you sitting up there."

With which she turned on her heel and skipped back across the lawn to Florrie and started to help lay out the plates.

His sister was maddening at times. But today he refused to be maddened. It was too good a day for a quarrel.

"It's my birthday," he shouted after her. "And I'm going to do just what I want."

Then he grinned. He was learning to stand up to Ellen in her nagging fits. It was simple. One just shouted at her and contradicted everything she said. In his triumph he strummed his heels against the wall and, in so doing, kicked the iron shaft of the long speaking tube which ran from his father's bedside, along the garden wall, through the surgery, over the stable roof and into Lambert, the groom's, attic window. The speaking tube let out an echoing iron boom.

"Ellen," shouted Rob peaceably. "Come and listen."

She stopped flouncing round the shimmering table cloth and looked back at him. He kicked the tube again, and the shaft thrummed and hummed all across the garden from the house to the surgery.

"Oh, Rob," she cried, entranced. "Do it again."

She ran back to the flower bed and looked at the speaking tube snaking along under the honeysuckle and the clematis, shuddering and booming each time he kicked it.

"Don't do it any more," she begged in sudden panic. "You might break it."

The speaking tube was a bond between them. They loved it. Two months ago when their father and Lambert were out in the dogcart visiting patients and their mother was out paying calls, Ellen had crept into their parents' bedroom and Rob had stationed himself outside the front door—for there was an extension of the speaking tube, which ran from the bedside down to a mouthpiece just above the doorbell. Rob had put his lips to this mouthpiece and blown an enormous blow.

"Goodness!" Ellen had shrieked from the other end. "What ever did you do?"

"I just blew."

"It sounded like a train whistling. It would have woken the dead."

That was the point of it, Rob thought. It had to waken Father when a patient wanted him in the middle of the night.

"Pretend you've had an accident," Ellen had suggested distantly from two floors up.

And Rob had groaned piteously while he had thought up something sufficiently dreadful. He had blown off his hand, he had wailed at last.

"Blown off your hand, my man! How ever did you do such a thing?"

"Been a-poachin', Doctor. That's what I done."

"Well, keep quiet and stay where you are," Ellen had announced in her bossy, practical way. "And I'll come down and sew it on again."

Today, with the shaft still shuddering faintly from Rob's kicks, they were both smitten with the same bewitching thought.

"Rob!" urged Ellen, her face alight with joy. "Let's . . . let's wait till after morning surgery. And then . . . and then . . ."

He gave the plan a moment's consideration and then shook his head.

"Lambert's driving Father into Norfolk. To Toft Monks," she wheedled. "I heard Father say so last night."

But Rob continued to shake his head.

"It's my birthday," he explained.

"But that's it! We'll never find a better chance. Mrs. Lambert's not in her cottage. She's in our kitchen, helping Cook."

"No," said Rob resolutely, turning aside from temptation. "Not today."

"You're afraid!" taunted Ellen.

"I'm not!" he roared, stung by her injustice.

"Then, why not today?"

He shrugged his shoulders angrily, turned his back on his sister and the garden, and stared out across Rushby Market Place, trying to sort out his thoughts. These were so private and complicated that he did not know how to put them into words—even to himself. It was his birthday. It had to be a *perfect* day. Nothing must go wrong. He could not bear being caught rummaging about in Mrs. Lambert's bedroom, where he had no right to be, and being sent to Father in disgrace. He did not want today to be filled with conspiracies and little flurries of fear. What with his party and his presents, it was going to be quite exciting enough as it was. And—for once in a way—the excitement was quite lawful and even smiled upon by his mother.

"You're a miserable spoilsport," Ellen hurled back at him before stalking off into the house in disgust.

Rob stared across the sunlit market square and slowly drifted into a comfortable summer dream in which he forgot

Ellen and her insults. It was comfortable because he had nearly consented to do something silly and had decided not to, instead; and this made him feel relieved—as though he had just escaped an accident; it also made him faintly pleased with himself. And it was a summer dream because everything about him reminded him of the season: the sunlight in his face, the warmth of the bricks between his thighs, and the smell of the early phlox in the flower bed below. If this was not enough, Rushby was full of farm laborers with faces as brown as hazel nuts, come into town to be bled by Dr. Tuttle before their sweating days in the harvest field. Mr. Crabbe, the druggist, had filled up his tank of leeches to the very top. Rob could see the tank, green and misty-looking, standing in the middle of the shop window across the street. He grinned at it with contentment. Leech weather meant birthday weather.

At this moment, an absentminded bee flew into his face, and he woke up with a start to see a stout little man leaping very oddly along the pavement immediately below him.

It was Mr. Brooks.

The draper had his head down and was looking intently at the squares of the paving stones. Rob recognized at once what he was doing, for he played that game himself. Mr. Brooks was avoiding walking on the lines.

"Mr. Brooks . . . Mr. Brooks," he called after him, suddenly overcome with anxiety. "You . . . you haven't forgotten?"

Mr. Brooks whirled around in the middle of a square as though he were a spinning top with a single leg—instead of an elderly man with two.

"*Forgotten,* Robert? Forgotten your birthday—and that I'm coming to your party this afternoon?"

Rob smiled his happy sheep smile.

"And you'll bring your white rabbit?"

The funny little man drew himself up to his full five feet two and suddenly looked as grave as he did on Sundays when he took around the plate in church.

"A magician doesn't *bring* his rabbit, Robert," he said severely. "He conjures it out of his hat."

Rob was not at all sure about this, but he did not like to say so, for he was beginning to be afraid that his friend might be really offended.

But he need not have worried.

"Bless me!" exclaimed Mr. Brooks, all twinkling smiles again. "But I *have* brought something—and I was forgetting all about it!"

And he started looking down into the bulging pocket of his alpaca coat and peering at something inside it.

"Steady there, steady," he crooned at the something in his pocket. "No need to be frightened. No need at all. Robert's a kind boy. A very kind boy."

And he gently lifted out a little creature with tawny fur and bright, frightened eyes.

"Oh, Mr. Brooks," breathed Rob in wonder. "Whatever is it?"

The little animal lay blinking in the sunlight, cupped in the draper's two hands. It had a sharp little snout, and its cheeks were puffed out as though it had mumps.

"It's a hamster."

Rob looked at the creature, entranced.

"I've never even heard of a hamster before," he said.

"Not likely you would," replied Mr. Brooks, smiling proudly. "They come from Syria and the Holy Land and

8

those parts. A friend of Professor Winthrop's over at Lowestoft brought a few back from Aleppo some ten years ago —and they've been breeding here ever since."

"And . . . and is this one for me?" he asked, hardly believing such a miracle possible.

Mr. Brooks nodded his head.

"Jump down off the wall, boy," he said, "and unlock the garden door. We'll put it in your brother's empty guinea-pig cage."

⩺ 2 ⩺

It was at lunch that this wonderful day began to go so terribly wrong.

"Robert," said Mother blandly. "I've invited Augustus Peebles this afternoon."

"Augustus!" exclaimed Rob in horror.

"Not *Augustus!*" exploded Ellen, showering her plate with crumbs of luncheon cake.

Rob grew scarlet in the face. He felt utterly outraged. He hated Augustus.

"But it's . . . it's *my* party, Mother," he burst out passionately, on the edge of tears. "You said . . . you said I could invite who I liked."

"Well, so you have."

"He didn't invite Augustus," protested Ellen. "Augustus is a horrid boy."

No grown-up ever realized how horrid he was.

"Don't interrupt, Ellen," said her mother sharply. "It has nothing to do with you."

Rob turned to his father.

"Must he come, Father? Must he really come?"

His father was crumbling a ginger biscuit on his plate and thoughtfully sipping his claret. Putting down his glass at last, he replied mildly:

"Hadn't you better listen to what your mother has to say?"

The Peebles were in great trouble, she explained. Little Charlotte was so very ill that everyone had to walk around the house on tiptoe.

"It's a sad sort of summer for Augustus."

"And is that why he's got to come to Rob's party?" asked Ellen tartly.

"I didn't go to *his* party when Ellen had measles," he said eagerly, clutching at a straw.

"Children! Children! How heartless you are!"

It was Mother who was heartless, thought Ellen. She had done a most cruel thing.

Rob, recognizing defeat, felt bitterly ill-used.

"It's all a cheat," he broke out. "It's not my party, after all."

"If you are going to lose your temper, Robert," said his mother severely, "then you had better leave the room."

Rob knew how his rages overtook him, and he turned to his father in anguish.

"But he's not going to lose his temper," said his father, smiling.

How could one little boy really spoil a party as wonderful as Robert's was going to be?

He felt himself grow calmer. Father was like that.

But he was not convinced.

Augustus could very well spoil his party, he grieved as he

trailed out into the garden after lunch and stared miserably at the table laid for tea.

Augustus could spoil heaven.

And spoil heaven is exactly what Augustus did.

All went well until after tea when they were playing hide and seek to while away the time until Mr. Brooks could shut up his shop and walk across the Market Place with his little collapsible conjuring table and his suitcase full of tricks.

"Fourteen, fifteen, sixteen," counted Ellen, hiding her eyes.

"Conjuring tricks are just the silly sort of things your family *would* have," whispered the evil-minded Augustus in Rob's ear.

By some dreadful mistake, they were both hiding behind the same clump of Aaron's rod.

"What do you mean?" asked Rob hoarsely, staring at him aghast.

"They're vulgar," sneered Augustus.

"They're not," shouted Rob, going scarlet in the face.

"Yes, they are. So's your whole family."

"They're not," shrieked Rob.

The pulse in his forehead was throbbing as though it would burst.

"Your father's nothing but an old sawbones," leered his horrible guest.

Rob did not know what a "sawbones" meant. And he did not even have time to guess. He was standing up, his arms flailing like a windmill.

"He's not. He's not. He's not," he screamed, punching Augustus's flabby face on the chin, on the nose, in the eyes.

Augustus howled; and then Rob cried out with pain, for

Augustus had begun defending himself with his fingernails.

"Stop! Stop!" cried Ellen, trying to tug Rob away.

"I won't," he sobbed angrily, giving Augustus another fistful on his chin.

"But you *must*," shouted Ellen.

"He . . . he called Father a 'sawbones,'" he muttered, panting to his sister through his clenched teeth as the blood trickled down his scratched cheek.

He could not bear Ellen not to understand. And he could not bear the other children to hear. "Sawbones" was something disgraceful. He was sure it was something disgraceful. It was a terrible, terrible taunt for Augustus to have made.

Stung again by the insult, he suddenly lowered his head and butted his enemy full in the stomach, so that Augustus flew straight out of the flower bed, rolled across the lawn, and disappeared under the trestle table.

"Robert! Robert!" thundered his father.

In the twinkling of an eye, he was lifted high in the air—above the dirty cups and saucers, above his screaming guests—and carried off into the house.

He lay on his bed, incredulous.

He could not believe it. He could not believe that such a terrible disaster had overtaken him.

His father had spanked him, drawn down the blinds, and left him to his hiccups.

"You've disgraced yourself, Robert," he had said coldly on leaving him. "You've disgraced us all."

It was the coldness that was so awful. He had never heard his father speak like that.

"I thought you were too old to behave so badly," he had said.

It was all a nightmare. It *must* be a nightmare. It was too horrible to be anything else. He prayed that he would wake up in a minute and find that none of it was true— that his father had not spoken like that, that Augustus had never come to his party—find, instead, that it was really early in the morning, before breakfast, and that his wonderful birthday had only just begun.

Yet, it was not so.

Suddenly he knew for certain that it was no dream, for looking down on the white sailor suit which his mother had made him wear, he saw that it was spotted with blood. At the sight of it, a terrible despair swept over him. His father despised him. He did not love him any more. In utter wretchedness, he longed to go to sleep and never wake up.

He wished he were dead.

He must really have slept, for ages and ages later he awoke to the glimmering shadows of his bedroom and saw that the sunlight was still dancing on the other side of the drawn blind. With an ache, he realized that something dreadful had happened, and while he was trying to recall what this dreadful something was, the sound of many people laughing floated up to him from the garden below.

"Goodness!" he thought. "It's my party! They're still at my party."

Too empty now to feel dumbfounded, he got to his feet, walked stiffly to the window, and peered down into the garden around the edge of the blind.

Mr. Brooks was doing his tricks, and his friends were sitting on the lawn in a circle at his feet. As another burst of laughter bounced up to his window, he saw that Mr. Brooks had pulled the white rabbit out of his top hat. The rabbit was whiffling its nose at them—as it always did.

Rob looked at the rabbit's nose and was stung by the terrible unfairness of it all. It was *his* party. *He* had invited Mr. Brooks. And there were his friends enjoying the fun that he had provided and forgetting all about him in disgrace upstairs. They had no right to be so happy. Mr. Brooks had no right to be doing his tricks. He had thought that Mr. Brooks had liked him. But he didn't. Nobody liked him. Nobody really cared about him at all.

Immediately below him, his parents were sitting on the garden seat, clapping their hands. The injustice of his father sitting there calmly as though nothing had happened filled him with cold fury. He suddenly hated him. He had tried to defend his father. And all he had earned was a horrible spanking and his father's contempt.

His cold rage grew and grew—like a huge genie slowly emerging from a Persian pot.

Nobody loved him. Not even his father.

He would run away—now—this very moment and find somewhere kinder to live.

As another burst of laughter exploded in the garden, Rob wiped his smudged eyes on the back of his hand, stole across the bedroom floor, and opened the door. Nobody would miss him, he thought, as he slipped down the front stairs. Nobody would mind when they found he had gone. And, even if they did, he would not care.

He fled across the empty Market Place, the shuttered shop windows turning blank eyes on his flight, and headed for the churchyard and the town steps that led down to the river. He would steal a boat, he thought, and row away. Go down to the sea, perhaps. Go to Germany or Denmark—or whatever country it was that one came to on the other side of the

North Sea. *Then* they'd be sorry, he told himself grimly. *Then* they'd see how unfair they'd all been.

He stood on the town wharf shivering, for there was Mr. Crabbe's rowboat moored to a bollard and swinging slightly on the full tide. It was all ready waiting for him—just as though it had known what had happened at his party. The oars had been left carelessly thrown down along the seat; the oarlocks and stretcher were in place. Only the rudder was missing. He shivered again. Stealing a boat was a dreadful thing to do. But this was a dreadful day. Nothing he did could make it much worse. So he stooped down, slipping the loop of the painter up off the bollard, pulled in the boat, and got into it carefully without jumping—just as his father had taught him. Then he settled himself on the thwart, lifted up the heavy oar, and pushed the boat off from the wharf.

He shivered again. Out in the middle of the river, he felt horribly exposed, for the ramparts of the town rose above the river, and people standing at their windows or looking over the churchyard wall would be able to see him alone in the boat in his childish white suit—alone and struggling with the oar. With an angry sob he managed at last to get it into the oarlock. But what was he to do now? One could not row a boat with only one oar. He would have to heave the other oar into place as well. But he had never rowed with two oars before. When Father had taken them on the river, Ellen had taken one and he had taken the other.

"Now, pull together," Father had shouted cheerfully. "The Henchmans are off to the Seven Seas."

"Seven Seas!" sobbed Rob as he heaved the second oar into its oarlock. "I'll really get to the Seven Seas this time. And then he'll never see me again."

He pulled a cumbrous stroke, appalled with the effort of rowing with two oars. And a new despair swept over him. He'd never get anywhere in Mr. Crabbe's stupid boat, he groaned. Some patient of his father's would see him from the bank and haul him back home in disgrace. He would get beaten for stealing—as well as for running away.

And then—in the middle of his despair—an extraordinary fact was borne in upon him. The riverside was deserted; there was nobody walking along the Churchyard Walk; nobody was looking out of his window.

"They're all sitting down eating shrimp teas," he thought with a pang.

And then another extraordinary thing occurred. When he glanced over the stern, he saw that the houses of Rushby were drifting away upstream at an astonishing speed. The town wharf had disappeared. Mr. Crabbe's boat was past the maltings already and going under the railway bridge. Peering over the gunwale to see what was the matter with the river, Rob saw that the tops of the weeds were languidly pointing downstream.

The tide had turned.

He stared at the weeds full of awe. So he was going to sea after all! The River Waveney and the boat and he himself were being hurried out of Rushby on the ebb tide. They'd be miles away in an hour. He sat with the grips of the oars tucked under his knees and the blades high in the air, dripping water, feeling very uneasy, for he was not used to having his wildest wishes so quickly fulfilled. It was eerie. It was as though some not very friendly magician had cast a spell on his affairs.

A cool evening wind slowly flattened the reeds on the

Norfolk bank and puckered the surface of the river into ripples. The ripples chuckled as they smacked against the prow of the boat.

Half an hour later, he was nearly two miles downstream, and Rushby church tower looked like a gray thumb in the sky. As he had drifted down the river, the whole horrible afternoon had become more and more of a jumble in his mind. He could not remember exactly what his father had said to him or what he himself had done. Only the terrible insult remained clear. He felt hot all over, for it had come to him what Augustus had meant. He had suddenly had a vision of Mr. Lark, the butcher, sawing off a sheep's knuckle-bone and throwing it out of his shop door to a dog waiting for it on the pavement. Sawbones, indeed! Likening his wonderful father to a butcher! He was so appalled by the taunt that he vowed that his father should never learn what Augustus had said. It would hurt him too much; and he could not bear that his father should be so hurt.

He shivered. Dusk was falling fast, and it was cold on the river. What was worse, the ebb tide was gaining strength, and the boat was gliding past the glistening willow roots and the ratholes in the bank at a frightening speed. Rob felt an intolerable ache. He did not want to go to sea. He wanted to go home instead, and comfort his father, somehow, for the terrible insult that he did not know that he had received. But he could not go home. He knew that he could never row Mr. Crabbe's heavy boat upstream against the ebb tide. He glanced about him in a little flurry of fear. The light had gone out of the sky and the river looked unfriendly; the ripples glinted sullenly as though they were made of steel.

"Still, I at least know where I am," he said aloud, trying to give himself some courage.

A clump of poplar trees had sailed past on the Norfolk bank. He and the boat were just entering Ashley Staithe reach.

The thought of Ashley Staithe made his intelligence wake up. If he could not row home against the tide, he could at least stop himself drifting any farther. He could paddle the boat over to the wharf and tie up for the night. Better still, he could pull the boat a little way up the dike where the kingfisher lived. It would be more secret there—and more sheltered. It would be easy. He'd clutch hold of the clumps of willow herb on the bank and float the boat up the dike that way. Then he would tie up and wait till the tide turned, and row back to Rushby on the flood. That the tide would not turn till after midnight was a thought that he pushed to the back of his mind.

Deep in the reedy shelter of the kingfisher dike, Rob pulled up the stretcher and settled down in the bottom of the boat. He lay looking at the deepening sky and at a star coming out, excited to be away from home so late at night and certain that such a going to bed as this would never come his way again, and yet frightened, too. He was frightened at what he had left behind at Rushby. It was terrible, really. He could not bear to think of it. Besides, he was continually being startled by the ploppings of water voles and the sudden croakings of moorhens. The marsh about him was everywhere alive.

Still, he was safe. He was sure he was safe. This was Ashley Staithe. And Ashley Staithe was a place of joy. They picnicked here every summer; they walked up from the river with the baskets and the kettle and built a fire near the old brickworks. It was a happy place. Even Mother said so. Nothing awful could happen to one at Ashley Staithe. So Rob lay at the bottom of the boat, staring at the star and thinking of William climbing up to the top of the brickkiln last summer and of Mr.

Emms, the kilnman, running out of his cottage and bellowing that William had got to come down quick. It wasn't safe. They were going to pull it down and build a new one.

"Why?" Ellen had shot at him.

" 'Cos we're a-goin' to start makin' bricks here agen. That's why, Miss."

"Funny," thought Rob sleepily at the bottom of the boat. The clay pits were all grown over with brambles.

When he woke up it was quite dark, and at first he could not think where he was. His shoulders ached, and the sides of the boat seemed to coffin him in. Then he heard a slight thrumming of water on the other side of the coffin boards and the soft, reedy sighing of the marsh. He knew where he was. He was at Ashley Staithe. He remembered everything. He remembered that he must get up and walk back to the river to see if the tide had turned.

A wind had blown up, and the stars were obscured by clouds. Down in the dike, the clumps of willow herb and hemp agrimony seemed to bend over him like the trees in a deep forest, and it was frighteningly dark. He felt a sharp twinge of fear. He would never find his way back to the river by land; he would miss the path and fall into a quagmire. The only thing he could see at all clearly was the dull light on the slapping water. He would have to untie the boat and go back down the dike the way he had come.

He hated this darkness. It made him feel lonely and small.

He wished Ellen were with him—or William—or his father.

He wished there were a light somewhere in all this blackness. Just a lamp in a cottage window. Just one bright star.

Yet, when he stood up in the boat, he saw that there *was* a kind of light, after all—for, looking away from the river in the direction of the old clay pits, he saw a strange orange plume, low in the sky. He clambered up on to the high bank of the dike and gaped at it in astonishment, for now the plume flattened itself over the top of the feathery reeds and now it spiraled up to a low cloud, turning the cloud orange, too. It was smoke. It was a column of tawny smoke.

What had happened? Was Mr. Emms's cottage on fire? But when there was a fire, he thought rapidly, people shouted and rang bells. That's what they did in Rushby. He stood on the bank, staring at the smoke and listening as hard as he could.

Not a sound came to him—save the murmurs of the marsh close at hand.

Rob was drawn to the wavering orange plume as a moth is drawn to an oil lamp. He felt bewitched. As he stumbled along the top of the bank, he was sure he was dreaming—or else that he was not at Ashley Staithe at all, but in another world quite different. When he came to the wide cart track which led up from the wharf to the old brickworks, he was certain that this was so, for the path was familiar—they had walked up it dozens of times with the picnic things—yet tonight it was not the same. It was magically changed. The ruts made by the cart wheels were deep black—they must go down to the center of the earth—and the mound in the middle was orange and warm and inviting. The prints of the horseshoes seemed to drag one's feet forward.

"So fairy tales are really true," he reflected in wonder. "I'm at Ashley Staithe in the middle of a fairy tale."

He looked down at himself to see if he had been altered, too. He saw that he was still wearing the hateful sailor suit; but it was orange, now. And the spots of blood were black. He frowned. He felt he looked foolish in this strange, new world.

As he drew nearer to the unearthly plume of light, he smelled the smoke and another sort of smell, which was new to him.

And then he heard a voice.

The voice startled him. It was both familiar and strange.

"More clay, Bill. Quick about it," said the voice.

It was Mr. Emms. But he was speaking very strangely. He seemed to be gasping.

"She's blowin', Jack," shouted another voice. "She's blowin' right at the top."

Rob ran around the last bend in the cart track and suddenly came to a full stop. Smoke was pouring out of the chimney of the brickkiln.

But it was not the smoke that astonished him so much. It was the brickkiln itself. At the top, the bricks were glowing—like a burning rose. And a man—Mr. Emms—was clambering right over this burning rose and gasping for help.

"More clay, Bill," he choked, as he plastered something black over the roseate glow. "Quick wi' it."

Rob never forgot the next dreadful few minutes.

He stepped out of the marsh and into the circle of light around the brickkiln at the very moment that the kilnman lost his footing and fell spread-eagled across the burning rose. Then, with a terrible cry, Mr. Emms fell twenty feet from the top of the kiln to the ground.

"Mr. Emms. Mr. Emms," cried Rob, running towards him.

"Jack," shouted the other man from the far side of the kiln. "Jack, what's the matter?"

Mr. Emms had fallen on his face. His leg was twisted sideways. His coat had a smoldering smell.

"Mr. Emms," wept Rob, tugging at the silent body.

When they turned him over, he groaned. He was burned on the palms of his hands.

"And he's broken his leg," muttered Bill.

Mrs. Emms had come running out of her cottage in her night things.

"I knew it. I knew it," she sobbed in anguish, as she tenderly

picked up one of his scorched hands. "He's too old for it. My Jack's too old for it."

Then she ran back to her cottage. She was going to fetch him a blanket, she said.

Bill glanced up from the groaning kilnman and stared at Rob.

"What you doin' here in the middle of the night?" he barked.

Rob felt so miserable about Mr. Emms that he could not be bothered to think about himself.

"I asked you what you was doin'," repeated the man savagely.

"Nothing much," Rob muttered.

He suddenly felt terribly guilty—as though it had somehow been *his* fault that Mr. Emms had fallen off the top of the brickkiln.

Mrs. Emms returned with the blanket and gently wrapped it over her husband. Then she looked up, seeing Rob clearly for the first time.

"It's one of Doctor Henchman's boys," she said absently, not really thinking about Rob or wondering why he was there.

"Dr. Henchman!" exclaimed the rough man. "It's Dr. Henchman we want here, Missus."

But how were they to get him, asked Mrs. Emms. It was five miles around by the road—and Mr. Jarman had taken the horse.

Mr. Emms groaned again.

"We did oughter get Dr. Henchman," muttered the grim man.

Rob looked down on the man and the woman, nervously twisting his fingers. Then he looked again at the unconscious Mr. Emms.

"I've . . . I've got a boat," he said hesitantly.

"A *boat?*" exclaimed Mrs. Emms. And she suddenly gave Rob her full attention. "A boat? Where've you got a boat?"

"In . . . in the kingfisher dike," he stammered.

As the grim man rowed Mr. Crabbe's boat fiercely upstream to Rushby, Rob felt the whole horrible day rushing back on him like a pianola roll spinning backwards on its spool. The stolen boat! His father's contempt! Augustus's bleeding nose! He tried to stop it. He tried to think only of poor Mr. Emms.

"What . . . what was Mr. Emms doing on top of the kiln?" he asked his shadowy companion.

They were firing the bricks in the kiln, he was told. But the pianola roll inside his head went on spinning. Spinning. Augustus had insulted his father. He had called him a sawbones. He, Rob, had stolen a boat.

"What was you a-doin' down in that ole dike?" asked the man at the oars.

When he had got down as far as Ashley Staithe, Rob explained, he had found he could not get back.

"The boat . . . the boat was too heavy," he said. "I . . . couldn't row it up against the tide."

Mr. Emms's mate digested this in silence for the whole of Boaters' Reach.

"Wonder he let you out in a boat alone," he rumbled out at last.

Now it was Rob's turn for silence. But the man seemed bent on an answer.

"Your father," he asked sharply. "Do he allow you on the river on your own?"

Rob sighed. He saw that a terrible retribution awaited him at home.

"Not really," he said apprehensively, noting that they were just about to shoot under the railway bridge.

It was dreadful how quickly the boat flew along under the man's oars. He could see the maltings now. The houses of Rushby towered up on his left. They were nearly back at the town wharf.

"You run for your father, boy," said the man as they drew alongside the quay. "I'll make the boat fast and follow."

Rob raced up the steep town steps, up, up, towards the looming parish church, his heart thumping and his brain in a muddle of separate facts. Mr. Emms was hurt. He was horribly hurt. He, Rob, had run away. He had stolen a boat. Through the churchyard he fled, clinging desperately in his thoughts to poor Mr. Emms. It was the middle of the night. Father would be in bed. He would run across the Market Place, race to the front door, and shout into the mouthpiece of the speaking tube.

"Wake up, Father! Please wake up. Mr. Emms has fallen off the top of the brickkiln."

But as he tore round the corner of the church tower and looked across the Market Place, he saw that nothing was as he had expected it to be. Every room in their house was lit up. Father was not in bed. Nobody was in bed. Even at Ellen's window there was a chink of light. He stared at his lighted home and gave a gasping sob. Father. Mother. Ellen. He suddenly realized what he had done to them all.

Shaken and frightened at what he had done, he realized in panic that his father might not be at home. He might be out on his horse looking for him. He decided to run past the front door and look in the stables to make sure. It was his father he wanted; not his mother. Besides, it was Father that Mr. Emms wanted.

As he headed past the garden wall, he saw a glimmering

light coming from the coach house. Father must be there. If not Father, then Lambert.

He heard voices.

"It's no good, sir," Lambert was saying. There was an odd gentleness in his voice. "We'll have to give over for tonight."

"Father, Father," Rob shouted, running into the stable yard. "There's been an accident."

His father whirled around, the carriage lamp still in his hand.

"Robert!" he sighed.

Rob had never seen his father look so gray and strained. His heart seemed to jump into his throat at the grayness.

"Robert, Robert," said his father.

Lambert had taken the lamp, and Father had lifted him up in his arms.

"My dear son. My dear son," he murmured, as he held him close to his prickly frieze cape.

Rob wanted to burst into tears.

"You've got to go to Ashley Staithe, Father," he gulped. "Mr. Emms has fallen off the brickkiln."

His father put him down but kept his hand on Rob's shoulder.

"All's well," he smiled uncertainly at Lambert. "And you'd better put the horse back in the dogcart."

Then he turned back to Rob.

"Now tell me more."

The words came out very oddly in a kind of croak.

"About Mr. Emms?"

His father nodded his head.

"He's broken his leg, I think. And he's . . . he's burned his hands."

The man who worked with him would be up from the river

in a minute. He'd tell him better . . . he'd . . . Rob stumbled on miserably, his heart aching not for Mr. Emms's grief but for his own.

"I'm . . . sorry. I'm so sorry, Father," he wept at last. "I didn't know it'd be like this."

The grip on his shoulder tightened.

"You know, Rob," came the quiet reply. "It's not such a very dreadful thing to be 'a sawbones.'"

Rob suddenly felt hot all over.

"Who told you?" he gasped in distress.

"Ellen."

Then an extraordinary thing happened. The tight grip on his shoulder relaxed. Very quietly, his father was laughing

They heard the sound of boots ringing across the midnight square.

"Bill Foulger, is that you?" called out his father.

The grim furnaceman strode into the shaft of light from the stable.

"Come into the surgery and help me pack up my things," he said.

Then he turned to Rob.

"Run quickly and tell your mother you're home."

Rob slipped through the open garden door and saw in the shadowy darkness that they had left the bare trestles still standing on the lawn. His heart began thumping uncomfortably. He trod especially quietly on the path. He did not want to face his mother. She would be cold with him. Contemptuous, even. He was sure she would. He turned the brass knob of the back door very gently so as to make no noise. Somehow he did not want her to hear him coming before he had actually arrived.

A lighted candle had been left on the passage table. Another glimmered in someone's hands halfway up the stairs.

"Rob," came a hoarse whisper.

It was Ellen.

They ran to meet each other so quickly that they collided on the bottom stair, and Ellen's candle went out.

"Oh, Rob, I'm so glad you're all right," she sighed in the pool of darkness. "I'm so terribly glad."

Her hands, touching his, were as cold as frogs. He felt deeply moved. She was in her nightdress. Her feet were bare. She must have been sitting on the stairs for hours and hours waiting for him to come home.

"Where did you go?" she whispered.

"I stole Mr. Crabbe's rowboat," he whispered back.

"You *what?*" she exclaimed out loud.

"Sh!"

The two words echoed like the report of a gun in the silent house.

"Ellen," called their mother from her bedroom. "Ellen, is that you?"

Rob shuddered. His mother's voice sounded oddly feeble and pathetic through the closed door.

"You must go to her," whispered Ellen. "Better get it over with."

He dragged his feet up the stairs. His mother was neither feeble nor pathetic. He knew this very well—just as he knew that once she had got over her relief that he was home she would begin to laugh cruelly at him and make him feel ridiculous.

On reaching the landing, he looked back down the well of the stairs at his sister. She had relit her candle from the one on

the passage table and stood looking up at him with a particularly Ellenish grin on her face. Seeing it, his spirits suddenly
rose. He felt almost breathless with delight. For he recognized
that grin. It was the one which, up to now, she had always re-
served for William.

Squaring his shoulders inside the stupid sailor suit and then
pausing a moment to square his chin, he knocked on his
mother's bedroom door.

Not the End of the World

≽ 1 ≼

It happened when she was twelve years old.

Looking back on that summer of 1893, Ellen Henchman realized that she had been expecting something dreadful to happen all along. She had felt it in her bones. The oddest of aches kept shooting down her shins.

"It's growing pains," her mother said. "I used to have them, too, when I was your age. You must go to bed earlier. And not run about so much."

Ellen sighed.

"That's not much of a cure!" she thought in despair.

But then, her mother's cures never *were* much good.

Ellen knew that it was her mind that ached quite as much as her legs, and lying in bed with nothing to do would make the ache in her mind grow worse and worse. She would have hours and hours to worry about Rob and William and herself.

They were changing. They were growing apart. That was the trouble. The three of them were shooting out sideways, like stars bursting out of a rocket. Panic-stricken at times, she could not imagine where she and her brothers were all going to come to earth.

"You'll feel better when we get to Walsingby," her father said, pinching her affectionately on the cheek. "Everyone's aches feel better by the sea."

Walsingby!

For a breathless moment, she was running along the beach with her hair streaming wild and the gulls screeching angrily over her head.

"Perhaps you are right," she said sadly, as she kissed him good night.

But she could not deceive herself. She did not think that even Walsingby could bring her back William.

"Ever since he's been at boarding school," she thought wretchedly, "William's been embarrassed by us all. He thinks Mother and Father are old-fashioned—and that Rob and I are just silly."

He no longer laughed at the things which Rob and she thought were funny. All the old jokes had gone stale. Worse still, she was sure that William was ashamed that she was his sister. She ached and ached. Not even Walsingby could make them the kind of friends that they used to be.

And Rob?

Well, Rob was impossible.

Ever since he had run away from home on his seventh birthday, he had been trying out his strength on them all.

Even their mother was losing her poise.

"It's high time that he joined William at St. Olaves," she had exclaimed in exasperation. "He needs to be knocked about by other boys."

And, for once, Ellen was inclined to agree with her.

But would Walsingby make Rob any easier to live with? She doubted it.

To make things worse, the day of their departure began with a row.

There was no help for it, their mother declared at breakfast. Rob's hamsters and white mice *smelled*. And that was the end of the matter.

"They *don't* smell," Rob stormed. "And if you won't let me take them, then *I* won't go either."

Their father lowered his *Times*.

"Mrs. Lambert has promised to feed them, Robert," he said quietly. "They'll be all right."

"No, they won't. They need *me*. They really do."

"Poor Rob," thought Ellen, surprised that she felt so sorry for him. It was not the pets that needed Rob, but Rob who needed his pets. He loved them. It was not fair of Mother to say that they smelled, for he watered and fed and cleaned them out most tenderly. He seemed born to take care of animals. He would miss his pets dreadfully at Walsingby. She was sure he would.

"You let me take them last year. And the year before," he said angrily.

"Well, they are *not* coming this year."

Their mother looked as immovable as Rushby church tower.

"You know, Robert," said his father, smiling a weary smile.

"Six hamsters and eight white mice *are* rather a lot for the inside of the brougham."

"But . . ."

"Shut up," snapped William.

So away they went, Lambert and Florrie, the parlormaid, perched up on the box, Rob and herself and their parents inside the stuffy brougham, and William pedaling behind on his safety bicycle, scowling in misery at his father's tin bath strapped nakedly to the roof of the carriage.

Ellen, shut up inside the brougham, was spared the spectacle of this ancient shame. Yet, she was scowling, too.

"I don't think families ought to be boxed up with one another like this for a whole hour—even though we *are* going to the sea," she told herself gloomily. "Rob's still mad about his pets. And Mother's only pretending to be calm. We're all too different. It's dangerous. One day we'll get mixed up really wrongly—like William's chemicals—and just explode."

She sat on the uncomfortable spring-back seat facing her parents and tried to think hopefully of the month ahead. She saw the huge sky arching over the sea and the low shore; she felt the tang of salt on her lips. And then she suddenly saw Etty.

Etty!

Etty was helping her to pick blackberries off a bush on Walsingby Common; they were giggling at each other because their lips were purple with squashed fruit.

How could she have forgotten Etty all these weary weeks?

The menace of things to come lifted like a sea scud.

Ellen squinted sideways at the furious Rob, lurching about

on the other spring-back seat—and suddenly wanted to laugh.

With Etty for her to play with, she could do without her brothers. William and Rob could go hang.

As they clattered into the farmyard, the hens scattered and a cock flew to the top of the manure heap and crowed.

"Hurray! We're here! We're here!" shouted Rob, bursting out of the brougham like a pea bursting out of a pod.

Their father got out next and turned to help their mother, who was taking her time—as she always did. Ellen watched her impatiently. Her mother was too regal for the country. She stood in the middle of the farmyard making formal little nods first to Father, then to William, and then to the hens, while she waited for Mr. and Mrs. Ransom to emerge from the kitchen door.

"Mr. Ransom! Mr. Ransom!" shouted Rob, hurling himself into the farmer's arms. "Where's Bessy? In the same sty?"

Ellen climbed out of the dark brougham and stood beside her mother, dazzled by the sunshine and smiling to feel the salt air fanning her cheek. Shading her eyes against the strong light, she saw Josiah, the donkey, grinning at her from the other side of the yard fence. She grinned back. Dear Walsingby! She sighed happily. Everything's the same!

Then, suddenly, she was aware that it was not.

"Where's Etty?" she asked Mrs. Ransom.

The farmer's wife looked at her sharply and then turned away, as though she had not heard her question. She was busy ushering Mother over the threshold.

"Where's Etty?" Ellen tackled her again, when they were alone in the kitchen.

Etty was a plowman's daughter who came up to the farm every summer "to help with the rough." She was fifteen, four-square, and friendly. And Ellen loved her.

"Etty Ling isn't coming anymore," Mrs. Ramson said flatly, her face shutting up like a trap.

"Not coming any more?" exclaimed Ellen in astonishment. "Why not?"

"Because I don't want her," replied Mrs. Ransom grimly. "It's as simple as that."

"But why don't you want her?" asked Ellen, growing more and more bewildered and angry.

Last summer Mrs. Ransom had declared that Etty was a treasure, a gem, a jewel beyond price. With all the extra work that the Henchman family brought with them, she didn't know what she would have done without Etty Ling.

"She's a mawther I'd 've been proud to name my own," she had told Ellen's mother.

Mrs. Ransom must have remembered this, too, for she turned away to push one of Mr. Ransom's dirty shirts into the copper.

"Etty's gone away, if you must know," she said sullenly.

"That's a lie," thought Ellen.

No one ever went away from Walsingby. You were born there, lived there, and—when the time came—were buried there, under a sandy mound in Walsingby churchyard. No one ever left the place, unless it was to go and fight in a war. And even Great-Uncle Tom, who had fought at Trafalgar, had returned to this farmhouse to die. Father's great-aunt Susan Henchman had never left the village; nor had the Cattermoles nor the Bobbits—let alone stay-at-home Etty Ling.

"She's gone up into Norfolk . . . to her mother's folk," continued Mrs. Ransom, blushing up the back of her neck.

Ellen fled from the kitchen, appalled.

Etty's mother had not come from Norfolk. She had been born at Dunthwaite, the village next door. Etty had told her so.

≫ 2 ≪

No one could understand why Ellen was so upset about Etty.

When she told William, he shrugged his shoulders and returned to cleaning the spokes of his safety bicycle. The shrug maddened her. It seemed to say: "Etty's only a girl. Why all the fuss?"

"She's my *friend*," Ellen shouted at him.

"Well, she's gone," he said, elbowing her out of the way as he wheeled his bicycle into the stable. "She's gone. And you'll have to make the best of it."

Rob was no better, for he could not even remember very clearly who Etty was. For a puzzled moment, he stopped scratching the sow between her ears with a pointed stick.

"Was she that fat girl who used to carry up the pails of water for Father's bath?"

The sow grunted for Rob to go on.

"Yes," snapped Ellen at them both.

"And who once tumbled in?"

Rob grinned. She wanted to clip him over the ear. For with Etty gone—vanished into nothing—the joke was no longer funny.

But her mother was the worst of all.

"I do not know what has happened to Etty," she told her daughter. "And I do not propose to ask."

"Why not?"

"Mrs. Ransom knows her own business."

Her mother was sitting on the hard, old-fashioned sofa in the farmhouse parlor, tidying the embroidery silks in her workbox. And she now motioned Ellen to sit down by her side. She obeyed, feeling glum—for a conference on the sofa with Mother always meant trouble.

"Besides, my dear," she continued, smiling her charming smile. "It was time that your friendship came to an end."

Ellen went scarlet in the face.

"Why?"

Mrs. Henchman explained that Etty Ling was only a plowman's daughter—a nice girl, yes, and a good worker. But hardly, hardly a suitable friend for Ellen.

"Why not?"

"My dear, what can you see in her? She's a simple country girl. She reads no books. She has not a thought in her head beyond the farm and her home and this village."

"I like her," said Ellen doggedly.

"And, Ellen dear, she speaks so roughly. Her accent is dreadful—really dreadful."

"I *like* it," maintained Ellen mulishly.

Outwardly, she looked flushed and rudely defiant. Inwardly, she wanted to howl.

Why did Mother keep calling her "dear"? Why had Mrs. Ransom told such dreadful lies? What had happened to Etty? Where was she? What had she done?

Bruised and shaken that first evening, Ellen went in search of her father. Dr. Henchman had fled from the confines of the brougham as speedily as the rest of them. He had seized his butterfly net, stuffed some glass-topped specimen boxes into the huge pockets of his holiday suit, and strode quickly away along the shore towards Dunthwaite.

Once down on the beach, Ellen saw him a long way off, stooping down over a patch of green herbage not far from Dunthwaite mere.

"That's ragwort," she thought. "And he's looking at the cinnabar caterpillars."

The sun had disappeared behind a bank of low cloud, and the sea, colorless and calm, crawled silently up the shingle and, as silently, crawled back again. It was like a sick beast. Gray sea. Gray sky. Shingle, dune, and mere. Walsingby was a somber place, without sun and wind—without Etty.

"Please, Father. Please help me," she begged over and over again in her mind as she crunched along the shingle towards the stooping figure.

But her father could not help her, either. He had not had time to realize that Etty was missing from the household.

"It's some women's squabble, very like," he suggested with a smile. "Mrs. Ransom has fallen out with Mrs. Ling."

"Nothing more?"

"I should not think so."

"Could you find out?"

Her father looked at her and laughed gently.

"I'll try, Ellen. But it won't be much good."

"What do you mean?"

"We Suffolk folk are a close and hidden race, my dear. We keep our secrets to ourselves."

"But . . . but they know you. You're a doctor."

"All the more reason, Ellen, why I should not poke my nose where it does not belong."

Next morning Ellen decided on a desperate measure: she would walk along the grassy lane leading from the farmyard, cross Walsingby Common, go down the muddy lane by the side of the estuary, and knock on the Lings' cottage door.

It was a desperate measure because she had never done such a thing before. Etty had never invited her back to her home—had seemed to shun all thought of Ellen ever meeting her parents and her brothers and sisters. It was strange really, now she came to think of it. The strangeness of it made her angry, for it proved that her mother might be right in saying that they came from different worlds. Etty had thought so, too.

She slipped out of the farmhouse, making sure that no one saw the direction she was taking, and then broke into a run, knowing that if she dawdled she might lose her courage altogether and turn tail before she had fulfilled her mission. Why should she feel so afraid? She did not know. Yet, for a reason that she could not understand, she felt like a spy crossing over the enemy lines under cover of dark. It was not dark. It was brilliantly light. The sunshine was falling out of the sky as harsh and sharp as splintered glass; it caught in the droplets from last night's scud, spangling the grass and the bracken fronds. It was a glorious day. Yet Ellen felt furtive and frightened and more than half ashamed of what she was about to do.

When she rounded the corner in the lane and first came within sight of the cottage, she took a deep breath—like someone about to make a high dive—and ran even faster.

A face glimmered in an upstairs window.

It was Etty. Ellen was sure it was Etty.

But, as she approached, the face disappeared, the windows looked eerily blank, and Etty's home, from its cheap slate roof to its scrub-worn threshold, transfixed her with a blind man's stare. Ellen shivered. In the garden there was neither a flower nor a weed to be seen; the potato ridges stretched relentlessly from the fence right up to the cottage wall.

"Goodness, what a bare, unfriendly place to live in," she thought, her heart beating fast as she rapped at the door.

This, to her surprise, immediately opened inwards, just as though she had given it a push; and a grim-faced woman stood in the dark space left in front of her.

"What do you want?" she rasped.

It frightened her that this horrible woman with her pinched mouth and her angry eyes had been silently waiting for her on the other side of the door.

"I . . . I came to see Etty."

"Well, Etty en't seein' yer. That's flat."

Ellen stood there dumbly, gazing at the wisps of hair escaping from Mrs. Ling's tight bun.

"Why not?" she burst out at last, her indignation getting the better of her surprise.

It was monstrous. Etty was her friend. Why was it such an awful thing to ask to see her?

"That's no business of yours, Miss Ellen," came the curt reply. "Now, be off with yer. And don't yer come 'ere agen."

And she closed the door in Ellen's face.

Angry and utterly bewildered, she stood staring at the blisters and scratches in the sun-bleached paint, hearing the bolts being pushed firmly home inside.

She sat for a long time afterwards deep in a bracken glade on the Common, waiting for her world to come back to itself. It was fresh there and clean-smelling; a place given over to rabbits and greenness. Above the bracken fronds arching over her head, a small white cloud was sailing across the blue.

Ellen felt at once outraged and full of guilt. She felt outraged because Mrs. Ling's cold anger with her had been so unexpected, so undeserved, so completely beyond understanding. And she felt guilty because she had poked her nose in where it had not belonged; she had poked it in despite her father's warning. She had been an intruder. A spy. And she had been found out and punished. Feeling terribly mortified and ashamed of herself, she pressed a green frond against her burning cheek and tried to give herself up to the sounds and sweet airs of Walsingby Common. Somewhere quite close to her a pheasant chick was stepping through the tall stems; a spider was running up her dress.

She loved this place. Nothing in her life must ever spoil it. Not even Etty.

"I'll just forget I've been to the cottage this morning," she told herself hopefully. "I'll just rub the whole thing off the slate."

☙ 3 ☚

Yet, try as hard as she could, she found it impossible to push her visit to the Lings out of her mind. Whatever she was doing, Etty's pale face kept glimmering at her from the upstairs window. She ran races with Rob along the shingle; she changed into her bathing costume among the tall tree lupines on the dunes and plunged into the cold, quiet sea; she walked for miles and miles across the saltings with Father and William, looking for the caterpillars of the Sand Dart Moth, which fed on the sea holly—for they wanted to see if they could rear them at home on slices of carrot in a biscuit box filled with sand. Ellen tried very hard to be interested in the caterpillars—and to forget that hateful first morning. But she could not. She was haunted by Etty. A terrible sense of foreboding weighed her down. Why had Mrs. Ransom and Mrs. Ling behaved so oddly? What was the *matter* with everyone at Walsingby?

"Still got those growing pains?" her father asked with a smile as they trudged back across the flat landscape to tea.

She had been lagging behind, dragging her feet in the sand.

She looked up. Only her father could help her, for only he could find out about Etty.

Then she shook her head. The guilt of her visit to the cottage stood between them. At the very thought of it, her cruel reception stung her afresh.

"She looks as though she's got a fever, Father," said William. "Her face is all hot."

"I'm perfectly all right," she snapped back at him.

She hated William at that moment. Brothers should not have eyes for what was going on in their sisters' minds.

Her father looked at her closely and then turned away and walked on. He was a good father. He never intruded.

And so the first week of their holiday trudged on. Only Rob and Father seemed entirely happy: Rob because Mr. Ransom had given him the care of one of his litters of pigs; and Father because Father, the naturalist, was clearly forgetting the anxieties of Father, the doctor, as he strode through the salt marshes, waving his butterfly net. William still looked bottled up with himself. And Mother hated Walsingby. She had always hated it.

"It's because Great-Uncle Tom used to swear awful naval oaths in the drawing room at Rushby," William had once confided to Ellen. "And Mother hates everything about the old man—even his farmhouse."

Ellen knew that her mother endured the month at the sea only for the sake of the rest of them—but she did not think this was because of the bluff old man, who had long been dead, but because her mother was really a "town person"—London born —and perhaps was not only bored but also a little frightened by the stark emptiness of the Suffolk coast.

As for Ellen herself, she awoke each morning to the gulls' cries and to the taste of salt on her lips and lay staring at the harsh light streaming through the gap in the curtains and slowly succumbed to the oppressive bewilderment of the day before.

"What's *happened* to Etty?" she asked herself anew. "Why

did Mrs. Ransom tell all those lies? Why was Mrs. Ling so cross?"

A horrible feeling that life and people were changing—that things were not at all as they had once seemed to be—clouded her mind. Nameless dreads hung about her like a swarm of gnats.

The sun shone. The sea sparkled. The white birds wheeled overhead. And on the dunes the dry pods of the wild lupines rasped in the light wind. Everything was the same. Yet the magic had gone.

The Saturday night after their arrival at Walsingby, Ellen was woken up by the sharp scrape of hobnailed boots on the cobblestones under her window. Someone banged with his knuckles on the kitchen door. She heard Mrs. Ransom grumble as she climbed slowly down the stairs; then she heard the bolts drawn back, a man's voice speaking excitedly about something, a smothered exclamation, and Mrs. Ransom running upstairs again in a hurry. She knocked on her parents' door.

"Dr. Henchman. Dr. Henchman," she called softly.

Ellen snuggled farther down her bed.

"Poor Father," she thought. "I'm so glad I'm not a doctor."

Scarcely a holiday at Walsingby went by that Father was not called out to some accident on the coast.

"It's too bad, Will!" their mother would exclaim angrily. "Can't they leave you alone just for one month in the year?"

Ellen listened for the wind. Not a leaf stirred in the walnut tree close by. There could not have been a wreck on such a quiet night. While her father dressed, she decided to leave the warmth of her bed and look out of the window. The great bowl of the sky was pricked with a thousand stars. She shivered with awe. Then, in idle curiosity, she glanced down into the yard at the light streaming out from the open kitchen door.

"Someone's probably got drunk at the *Duke of York*," she thought as she climbed back under the blankets. "And he's fallen off his horse on the way home."

Ellen's imagination was peopled with drunkards falling off horses or knocking one another about in tipsy brawls, for drunkenness was the only adult sin of which she had a close knowledge. She knew vaguely that grown-ups sometimes forged five-pound notes and robbed banks and, sometimes, even murdered one another. But these were rare and far-off things. At home at Rushby, drunkenness rolled swearing across the Market Place and tumbled over the front doorstep. Father was for ever going out and bandaging it up.

Next morning Dr. Henchman was still not home by breakfast time.

"Goodness, Father must be hungry!" Rob exclaimed between one spoonful of porridge and the next.

"What was it, Mother? An accident?" asked William.

"I do not know, William," their mother replied shortly, pursing her lips in a way that meant: "No further questions are to be asked. The matter is closed."

Ellen sighed and helped herself to Demerara sugar. She was used to such heavy secrecy; they were all used to it. It was part of the price of being the children of a doctor.

Yet nothing in their training had prepared them for what followed.

The morning room at Great-Uncle Tom's farmhouse led out of the parlor; and the breakfast table at which the three of them were sitting was placed in the window of the morning room, so that while they could all see out into the garden, not one of them could either see or be seen by anyone coming into the parlor from the front door.

Just after Mrs. Ransom had brought them their bacon and eggs, Ellen heard their father's step in the outer hall. Their mother rose quickly and walked into the parlor to greet him.

"Cara! Cara!" he called out, as he came along the passage.

Something in the tone of his voice riveted their attention. He sounded terribly weary and unlike himself.

"Oh, my dear, my dear," he broke out, coming to her. "The hardness of their hearts! The cruelty of it all!"

"Hush, Will. Hush, my dear," they heard their mother whisper urgently. "The children. They're in the morning room."

The two of them murmured together, their father in grief, their mother trying to console him.

Ellen and Rob and William looked at each other in white-faced astonishment. They had never heard their father speak in such distress. He was always the calmest and happiest of men.

"What does he mean?" whispered Rob, as his parents walked out of the parlor and into the garden. "Who's been so cruel?"

"Don't know," replied Ellen, too shocked by her father's despair to be able to think properly.

Rob turned to William, but he only shook his head.

And then Ellen shuddered.

What terrible deed had been done along the coast to cause him such grief?

The eggs grew cold and glassy-eyed on their plates as the three of them turned and stared out of the window at their parents walking arm in arm at the far end of the garden behind the raspberry canes. Their mother was looking up into their father's face with an expression of love and concern that Ellen had never seen before. It was a fresh shock. Mother must really love Father, after all. They must have a secret sort of understanding which they had kept hidden from their children.

Ellen watched her mother with mounting resentment. Her mother had no right to be able to comfort Father in that way. She had no right to take his hand and press it against her cheek. She had no right to charm the weary angriness out of his face. And then she realized with a fresh shock that she— Ellen—was jealous. Jealous of her own mother!

"Goodness, you crybaby," William said scornfully to her. "There's no need to burst into tears. Father's just worried about a case. That's all."

"I've never seen him worried about a case like *that*," said Rob ruminatively—and not very happily. "I never have."

Slowly the family righted itself and continued their holiday on a more even keel. Their father regained his calm; the sad and angry lines chiseled around his mouth disappeared. He took to walking off by himself for an hour every morning, but there was nothing new in this. He had done it in other years. After the crowded hurry of his life at Rushby, he needed a little solitude. Ellen understood his need. They all did—even Rob.

As for themselves, their parents seemed more concerned than usual that they should all have plenty to do. William and Rob went to sea for the day with the men of the Walsingby trawler. Ellen discovered a copy of *Mr. Midshipman Easy* in the parlor bookshelf with Great-Uncle Tom's signature scrawled across the flyleaf and escaped with it to the dunes all morning for a long read among the lupines, undisturbed by her mother. In a spell of fine weather, they took a picnic to Ness Castle, perched up on its low and crumbling cliff. And the following morning the brougham was ordered to drive them all to Framlingham to visit the great Tudor tombs in the parish church.

"They seem awfully anxious that we should *learn* things," grumbled Rob into Ellen's ear as they stood staring incuriously at the alabaster monument to the Earl of Surrey, listening with half an ear to their mother reading out of the guidebook.

Ellen knew that Rob was longing to get back to his pigs.

"Well, at least he had his head cut off," she said to cheer him up.

"I wonder how many hacks it took to do it," he mused ghoulishly.

"Don't be horrible," she hissed back. "You're a disgusting child."

Yet he was not disgusting really, she came to think later, as she walked around the shadowy aisled chancel and peered at one somber tomb after another and heard her mother recite the terrible tale of religious persecution and the treachery of kings. Rob was a realist. She came out into the sunlight of Framlingham churchyard and blinked at the grassy mounds and the weathered headstones—and suddenly shivered.

"And now, what about stopping for tea at *The Lord Howard Arms* on the way home?" asked their father, smiling cheerfully at the prospect.

"Stop at a *hotel?*" exclaimed William, hardly believing their good luck.

They had never done such a thing before.

Their father nodded.

"Oh, good! How wonderful!" shouted Rob, skipping gaily down the churchyard path.

Yet, in spite of the distractions which her parents provided, Ellen came back in the evenings to her own particular ache: What had happened to Etty? Why had Mrs. Ransom told her a clumsy lie? Why had Mrs. Ling been so angry with her? And —nearer home, how was it that she had never recognized the secret understanding between her parents before? Everything disturbed her: Father, Mother, William, Rob, Walsingby—they were all changing form and flying out of her reach.

≫ 4 ≪

Ten days after their father's startling outburst, their mother swept down the shabby stairs in her green and crimson ottoman silk dress and ordered Florrie to brush their father's top hat.

"Children," she anounced. "Your father and I have been invited to luncheon with Colonel and Mrs. Stacey-Cunningham at Eastwold Hall. We shall be away all day."

She wanted them to behave, she said, not to give the Ransoms any trouble, and to occupy themselves sensibly—with a long walk, or something.

"You might take them over to Dunthwaite, William," their father suggested. "I could do with a fresh supply of sea holly for the caterpillars."

"Poor Father!" thought Ellen. "He does not want to be dressed up in his frock coat and that dreadful high collar when he's on holiday. He wants to stay at home and peer through his microscope."

But it was Mother's great day. Her pleased little smile told them all as much. She stepped towards the waiting brougham nodding last-minute commands first to right and then to left.

"Yes, look after the two of them, William," she said. "And see that they do what you say."

Rob looked mutinous but held his tongue. Ellen sighed with relief: they had at least not been left in charge of Florrie. And poor William nodded his head and looked thoroughly uncomfortable. He took no pride in being his mother's favorite—and the eldest of the three.

"I'm not going to Dunthwaite," said Rob decisively, as soon as the brougham had disappeared down the lane. "I've got work of my own to do."

"What?"

William never wasted words.

"Helping Mr. Ransom move the pigpen."

"Has he asked you to help him?"

"Yes."

It seemed sensible to leave him to his task, so William and Ellen set off down the coast on their own.

It was a blue and golden day. Perfect Walsingby weather, Ellen remembered long afterwards. A soft wind blew in their faces from the south, and as she saw the terns darting over the curling waves and heard the lupine pods singing in the dunes, her spirits rose; she felt almost happy. She glanced secretly at her brother to see if he was feeling happier, too. Then she smiled. William was looking more friendly than of late—less hidden. She walked on, savoring this friendliness in silence, fearing to blunder into speech.

"Funny!" she thought, as they clumped on together over the shingle to the mere with the feeling of friendliness growing stronger with every hundred yards. "Funny! One can talk with a brother without saying a single word."

They gathered a basket of sea-holly leaves and then sat down to eat the bread and cheese and the slices of luncheon cake which Mrs. Ransom had prepared for them.

"Wonder where Rob's having his lunch," said Ellen.

"With his pigs—if he's been given his choice," grinned William.

It was on the way home that they saw her—standing waist-high among the lupines.

"William!" exclaimed Ellen. "It's Etty!"

William shaded his eyes, for they were still a long way off.

"She's seen us," he said in a puzzled voice. "I'm sure she turned around and saw us."

"And now she's disappeared," said Ellen, equally non-plussed.

They raked the length of the sand dunes with their eyes. The light wind was running wild in the lupine bushes, now flattening and now frisking out the leaves, so that the whole ridge seemed in perpetual motion, dimpling now whitish-green and now emerald. It was a confusing sight, and Ellen kept imagining that she saw her friend where she was not.

"I don't know why we're running," William panted after her. "It's clear that she doesn't want us to talk to her."

Ellen could not understand it. Etty was her friend.

"There she is!" she exclaimed triumphantly, forgetting her bewilderment.

They had rounded a spur of blown sand, and there was Etty standing just below the top of the ridge. There was something terribly wrong. Her shoulders drooped, and she held her hands over her face in an attitude of utter despair.

"Etty!" shouted Ellen, floundering over the tussocks of marram grass. "Etty, what's the matter?"

The girl dropped her hands and stood quite still, staring at them in a white-faced, hopeless kind of way.

"Etty," panted Ellen, as she reached her at last. "What's happened?"

Etty looked dreadful. Her hair was wild, and great dark shadows ringed her eyes. She appeared both frenzied and ill.

"I've lost it," she whispered in horror. "I've lost it."

"What have you lost?" asked Ellen.

But Etty did not seem to hear. She began rocking slowly from one foot to the other.

"I've lost it," she repeated dully, as though she were talking just to herself. "I've lost it."

"Tell us *what* you have lost," demanded William.

His voice came out sharp and stern and extraordinarily loud. It startled all three of them.

Etty gave a little shudder and tried to focus William in her gaze.

"The baby," she sighed at last.

"A *baby?*" shouted Ellen in astonishment.

William went very white in the face.

"Do you mean it's dead?" he asked.

Etty burst into a storm of tears.

No, the baby was not dead, she sobbed. It was well. It was very well. But she could not find it. And she put her hands over her face again and cried and cried.

Ellen could not understand it at all.

"Do you mean someone's put it down somewhere—and you don't know where?"

The wretched Etty nodded her head.

And then William did a very odd thing. He snatched Etty's hands away from her face and gave her a violent shake.

"William!" gasped Ellen.

"Now, tell us about the baby, Etty," he said fiercely.

Etty stopped crying in the very middle of a huge sob and gave a kind of hiccup, instead. And then, in broken, incoherent sentences, she told her miserable tale.

She had brought the baby down to the shore in the morning, she said. And then . . . and then . . . she had remembered something at home. It was fresh and nice on the beach, she explained, and the baby had smiled and seemed to like it. So . . . so she had found a sheltered hollow in the dunes . . . among the lupines . . . out of the wind . . . and . . . scooped a little nest in the sand for it.

"And . . . and I left it there," she said, beginning to cry again.

"And now you can't find where you left it?" asked William.

Etty nodded her head, speechless with sobs.

"Don't cry, Etty, please don't cry," said Ellen. "William and I will help you to look for it. We're bound to find it. Please don't cry."

Etty wailed that she had been looking for the baby for a whole hour. It was gone. It had vanished.

William and Ellen looked along the mile-long stretch of lupine-covered dune.

"You've mistaken the place, that's all," said William in a calm voice. "It's very easily done. One sandy hollow looks just like the next."

"We'll fan out," said Ellen, trying to be consoling. "Just like the beaters do at pheasant time."

Before they did so, William made Etty describe as nearly as she could what she remembered about the hollow that she had chosen. Was it a hundred yards, four hundred yards, or more from the farm? Etty shook her head miserably; she knew nothing about hundreds of yards. Did the hollow face the sea? Yes, Etty thought it did. Was there marram grass growing near? Or a horned poppy? Or anything special that she could remember?

Etty shook her head and began weeping again.

"Poor Etty," said Ellen in deep distress for her friend. "I do understand how you feel. Your mother will be so cross with you for losing her baby."

William suddenly went scarlet in the face.

"Come along, Ellen," he said sharply. "You take the shore side of the ridge. Etty and I will comb along the top."

Ellen glanced up at her brother in surprise; he had suddenly sounded so cross. Then, feeling aggrieved, she did as she was bid. Brothers, she thought, were very odd in the way they reacted to what their sisters said. In fact, William was behaving in a very odd manner altogether. She had never known him before to take charge of people with such authority.

Her eyes swept from left to right in a sweep that took in lupine bushes, sandy hollow, marram grass, shingle, flotsam, and gently breaking waves. Then, back again they went: spray, wet shingle, spars, marram grass, and sandy hollow.

"Well, the baby has not been washed out to sea. That's one good thing," she thought.

The wrack left by the high tide snaked across the beach in an untidy rim at least twenty yards from the nearest spur of the dunes. Besides, the tide was still going out.

"What was the baby wearing?" she called up to Etty.

It might be easier not to pass the baby by if she knew what color to look for.

The question caused great distress. Etty burst into tears again.

The baby was wrapped up in her red flannel petticoat, she sobbed. A red flannel petticoat! Ellen felt like bursting into tears, too. If Etty had really been looking for the baby for a whole hour, how could she possibly have failed to notice such a conspicuous-colored bundle? It was impossible. Someone must have *taken* the child. Stolen it. Ellen trudged on in despair. Sandy hollow; shingle; sea. Sea; shingle; sandy hollow. Everything blurred in front of her eyes. It was dreadful. Too dreadful. Someone must have kidnapped the baby.

When she was upset about something, Ellen often closed her eyes for a moment; it helped her to regain her balance. She did so now. As she stood there on the edge of the beach with sight shut out, she was slowly made aware of the sounds of the Suffolk shore: the soft thud and hiss of the breaking surf; the light jingle of the small stones drawn back with the waves; the mournful mewing of the herring gulls.

Gulls!

She opened her eyes and looked up at the beautiful birds sailing serenely across the blue—high above her head—and was suddenly struck by a terrifying thought. The herring gulls were not always as composed as this. Sometimes they swooped in anger, barking like fierce dogs. Could a herring gull have snatched up Mrs. Ling's baby? She looked up at the top of the ridge and longed to ask Etty how big the baby was, but knowing the horrible idea that haunted her she did not dare to ask.

Then she knew that she had been a fool. It was eagles who snatched up babies, not gulls.

They had come now to the end of the dunes. Great-Uncle Tom's cattle pasture lay only fifty yards ahead. The three of them looked at one another, white-faced and despairing.

"We'd better get help from the farm," Ellen suggested.

At this, Etty burst into frenzied sobs.

"No. No. Please don't," she cried, clutching at William to prevent him from going. She seemed beside herself with anguish.

"But of course someone must go," said Ellen, greatly puzzled. "Someone must raise the alarm."

Etty flung herself into William's arms, utterly distraught.

William, looking embarrassed but not flustered, nodded to Ellen over the girl's shoulder.

"You go," he mouthed at his sister.

And Ellen fled through the pasture and up the lane.

Two years ago, when she had just learned to swim, Ellen had found herself, while out bathing one morning, standing up to her waist in the sea some ten yards from the shore, staring in horror at a great rogue wave moving quickly and relentlessly towards her. There had been no time to run back to the beach. She had had to stand her ground—terrified—while the huge green monster arched over her head. She had taken a deep breath and had prayed that she was not about to die. In the event, she had been tossed over and over by the breaking wave, had swallowed a great deal of water, and had finally picked herself up, feeling furiously angry with the sea.

That afternoon, as she ran towards the farm, she felt that another rogue wave was about to break over her head; but whereas that first terror of two years ago had had a shape and a color and a taste, this present one was like something sensed in a nightmare: a being without form. Mrs. Ling's baby had been stolen. That was bad enough. But behind this tragic mischance loomed something far worse which Ellen could not begin to explain to herself—a terrible menace beyond her understanding.

The stackyard was deserted, and so were the milking sheds. Ellen realized that Mr. Ransom must have decided to start cutting the wheat in the forty-acre field after all. She ran past a tumbledown shed that had once been used to stable the donkey and was about to race across the farmyard to Mrs. Ransom's kitchen door when she suddenly slackened her pace, stopped, listened, and then returned much puzzled to the donkey house. A strange little mewing was coming from inside.

Then her heart gave an uncomfortable lurch. The sound suddenly took her back to the nursery at Rushby after Rob was born. She plunged through the nettles and tore open the battered wooden door.

"Rob!" she gasped.

Rob was crouching on the ground in front of a crying, red-flanneled bundle laid out on a bedding of hay.

"Rob! What are you doing?"

Rob looked up at her, both shamefaced and indignant.

"Can't you see," he said. "I'm trying to feed a baby."

He had a mug of milk and a slice of luncheon cake beside him on the ground.

"But it's Mrs. Ling's baby!" Ellen cried out, suddenly furiously angry with him. "How *could* you do such a thing?"

"The baby's been thrown away," Rob defended himself loudly over the squalls of the unhappy bundle.

"It hadn't. It hadn't. How can you say such a thing?"

"It was in a hole in the sand. It was half covered with lupine leaves."

"Etty was coming back."

"How was I to know?"

"But you can't just take babies home like that. It's a wicked thing to do."

Rob looked up at her, deeply offended.

"Pharaoh's daughter did," he replied with dignity.

Ellen gasped.

"But you're not Pharaoh's daughter."

The red bundle gave a piteous mew.

"And that's not Moses," she added. "It's Mrs. Ling's baby."

The little creature's face was contorted with rage.

"It's hungry," said Rob urgently, moistening a small pellet of dry cake in the milk and pushing the sop into the blindly groping mouth.

"That's not the way to feed a baby," said Ellen scornfully, stooping down to pick it up. "You must hold it in your arms."

"No!" cried Rob fiercely, pushing her away. "It's my job. I found it."

They stared at each other, Rob crouching over the nest of hay, Ellen longing to pick the child up—bitterly angry across the sexes.

And then Ellen suddenly pulled herself together.

Etty!

Poor Etty was still distraught with grief.

"You must go and tell her, Rob, that you've taken the child. She's on the edge of the dunes—with William."

"You go."

There was no need for either of them to go, for while they argued they heard the sound of footsteps on the path outside the shed and Etty's hopeless sobs.

"Etty," Ellen shouted, bursting out into the sunlight. "The baby's here. Rob's got it."

Etty tore straight through a tall clump of nettles, pushed Ellen aside and snatched up the baby with the speed and ferocity of a tigress.

William and Ellen and Rob stood gaping at her—utterly dumbfounded—for she was clutching the baby in her arms and covering its face and hands with kisses. She was crooning to it. She was smiling. Oblivious of everything but the baby's need, she was tearing the buttons in her bodice undone.

Ellen suddenly gasped with astonishment. The rogue wave had broken over her head.

It was Etty's own baby. Not her mother's.

She closed her eyes. The known world was toppling to the ground on every side. How *could* it be Etty's baby? Etty had no husband. And then, in the darkness, she saw Mrs. Ling's coarse and angry face at the cottage door and, more dreadful still—the scooped-out hollow in the sand half-covered over with lupine leaves. She shuddered.

"Hush!" whispered Rob.

She opened her eyes again, and the four of them listened, white-faced, to the clop, clop of a horse and the rattle of the brougham approaching along the lane.

"They've come back," whispered William.

Each one of them stood fearbound, listening to the brougham drive up to the front door. Ellen heard Lambert jump down from the box and open the carriage door and her mother saying something short and serious to her father as she walked up the steps into the house.

"They're all inside," said Rob, breathing more calmly.

"You'd better go home, Etty," said William. "I'll see you across the Common."

They emerged from the darkness of the donkey house, one by one, to find Dr. Henchman just outside, examining the bruised nettles for caterpillars.

"Ah William, Rob, Ellen!" he exclaimed in surprise. "And Etty! Etty, I was going to call on you this evening."

He looked searchingly at his three children, pondered something in his mind, and then shrugged his shoulders.

"Etty," he said, smiling. "Mrs. Henchman and I drove around by your aunt at Cove Hythe on our way home. She says she'll have you both."

Etty looked at him in astonishment.

"My Aunt Alma?"

"Yes, didn't you know? Didn't your mother tell you that I was going to ask your aunt?"

Etty shook her head. Tears the size of small marbles were rolling slowly down her cheeks.

"She's glad to have you," he continued cheerfully. "She'll give you both a good home."

Etty broke down completely, weeping—not hopelessly as before—but in sheer relief.

"I like my Aunt Alma," she sobbed. "She's a good 'un."

Then her father turned to Ellen.

"Your mother wants to see you in the parlor, Ellen. She's waiting for you. You had better go."

As Ellen left them, full of foreboding, she heard her father exclaim:

"Goodness! Who's been giving that poor child Mrs. Ransom's currant cake?"

≥ 5 ≤

Ellen found her mother sitting on the parlor sofa, looking utterly unlike herself. She was pink in the face with embarrassment.

"Ellen," she said, beckoning her daughter to sit on the sofa beside her, "you are very young to be told these things . . . but . . . but I think it is time that . . . that you should be told the facts of life."

Dazed by all that had happened, Ellen sat down and lifted her eyes inquiringly to her mother's face. Then she glanced away quickly, for her mother was not looking at her. She was staring unseeingly out of the window, instead, and trembling. Her mother was trembling! She could not understand it at all.

Slowly, and with long pauses between her sentences, her mother began telling her about the bees and flowers. Ellen stared blankly at the cameo brooch pinned to the bosom of the ottoman silk dress and wondered what she was trying to say.

Her thought wandered back to Etty. Etty crying. Etty in despair. Etty standing in the donkey-house, clutching the baby and kissing its screwed-up face and hands.

"Ellen!" exclaimed her mother sharply. "You have not been listening to a word I have said!"

She shook her head.

"Etty's had a baby," she blurted out.

Her mother nodded grimly.

"And Mrs. Ling is very angry with her?"

"Of *course,* she is very angry with her!"

Her mother's mouth looked tight and hard.

Overwhelmed by the anguish of this confirmation, Ellen fled from the room. She ran and ran, out of the door, through the farmyard, down the lane, across the cattle pasture, and out into the beach. Choosing the deepest hollow in the sand dunes and the tallest clump of lupines she could find, she flung herself down and wept.

A thousand ages later, Rob appeared on the skyline, walking along the top of the ridge.

"Hallo, Ellen," he shouted down gaily. "I thought I'd find you somewhere here."

He ran down the slope towards her in a flurry of sand.

"Father says you have to mix cows' milk with sugar and water to feed babies with. Did you know?"

Ellen looked at him dully and shook her head.

"He thought I'd better know, just in case I found another baby lying about."

Having retailed this new piece of information, he ran off and left her. And Ellen continued to sit in her private hollow and stare miserably out to sea.

Lying around! The baby left lying around! That was the most awful part of it all!

It had started to rain before William found her.

"Rob said you were here," he said laconically, sitting down beside her and following her gaze to the sea.

Ellen turned to him at last, the rain running down her face. He looked pinched and white and as wet as herself.

"Oh, William," she burst out. "I can't bear it. Etty tried to *abandon* the baby. Didn't she?"

William looked round at her and nodded. But, as he did so, a warmth seemed to creep slowly across his taut face.

"But she came back for it," he said, with a smile beginning to dawn in his eyes. "She came back for it, Ellen. She loves it. She loves the baby. You saw how she loves it."

Ellen felt a suffocating weight slowly lifting from her chest.

"It's not the end of the world," he said, looking at her tear-stained face. "She's got the baby. She's got a home for it."

Suddenly, and for the merest moment, Ellen saw that William looked just like Father.

She gave a long-drawn sigh of relief.

"No. It's not the end of the world," she murmured.

The Zenana
Mission Bazaar

≥ 1 ≤

Two years later, Mrs. Henchman could not conceal her disappointment at the way in which her three children were turning out. They were "neither fish, fowl, nor good red herring." William's voice wobbled between man's and boy's; Ellen had straggled up into a long-legged, awkward girl; and Robert, at eleven, had grown more wayward and willful than ever.

"Such *pretty* little children they used to be," she sighed to her husband, remembering their clean and starched appearance when Nurse brought them down to the drawing room after nursery tea.

"Have patience, Cara," the good doctor replied, smiling his

weary smile. "Do not despair. They will grow up to do you credit—in time."

But what a time!

After the disastrous affair of the Zenana Mission Bazaar, it looked as though they might both have to wait for the millennium.

"My dears," said Aunt Mary, smiling at her niece and two nephews over the pile of toasted muffins. "It is going to be an especially wonderful bazaar this year. Now, eat up the muffins quickly—while they are still hot. And I'll tell you why."

She explained that the India mission wanted to build a dispensary at Taralpur and was appealing for greater efforts in raising money from its friends at home.

"I know that that is an old story," she said, her eyes twinkling. "Missionaries are always asking for money. But your Uncle John has visited Taralpur himself. He says that conditions are very bad. Here is his letter. 'I have seen women crouching in the dust all day around Miss Drury's tent,' he writes. 'Hundreds of them—all seeking medical attention. Miss Drury is short of drugs, instruments—even basins. But, worst of all, she is short of space. With a mere £400 we could build her a fine, mud-walled dispensary with glazed windows to keep out the dust and a wide veranda, where the poor women could wait out of the glare of the sun.'"

"Oh, good!" exclaimed Rob, with his mouth full of muffin. "That sounds a much better idea."

"Of course, it is!" said Aunt Mary eagerly. "A tent must be dreadfully unhygienic for medical work. And so hot for Miss Drury."

"No, I didn't mean that," Rob insisted. "I meant it was much better to build a dispensary than to teach all those zenana girls things they don't want to learn."

Ellen gave Rob a kick under the table. Bringing light into dark places was Aunt Mary's life's work.

"What makes you think those poor ignorant girls do not want to learn?" their aunt asked.

She did not sound offended—merely curious.

"It's all in the missionary magazine," blurted out Rob. "They're much happier lying about on cushions and ottomans eating their sweetmeats than learning to read."

Ellen and William looked at each other and rolled up their eyes in despair. They prayed that Rob was not going to involve them in his heresy, for they, too, had read the articles in the missionary magazine and come to the same conclusion.

"It sounds such fun in the zenana," continued the oblivious Rob. "None of that awful algebra that Ellen hates so much. Just laughing and singing and jangling one's bangles and earrings about and playing with the white cockatoos in the cages over one's head."

"And do you think your sister would be content with just *that?*" their aunt darted at him. "Shut up and never allowed to go out? Never to go to market or walk in the country?" Never to be able to read Scott's novels and *Little Women?*"

"No, I *wouldn't!*" exclaimed Ellen.

"Well, now, Rob," continued Aunt Mary with a twinkle as she picked up the toasting fork to prod another muffin to toast. "Why should not the women of India have a chance to lead the purposeful lives that Ellen and I lead here?"

Neither Rob nor Ellen was quite sure that Ellen *did* lead a purposeful life, but Rob did not dispute the point. He just grinned an acknowledgment of his defeat and then began licking the hot butter off his fingers.

Ellen kicked him again under the table.

"Use your handkerchief, you disgusting thing," she hissed.

Yet, intent though she appeared on the family manners, her heart was singing with joy. It was always like this with Aunt Mary. Storm clouds that would have broken in lightning and deluged rain in Mother's drawing room somehow blew away to nothing in Aunt Mary's house. Aunt Mary was a great blessing to them all. She was clever and upright and ugly— and as tender as a rose. It was strange that she was so ugly, Ellen often thought, for her face was very like their father's; but whereas the straight brows, the firm nose, and the wide mouth looked strong and handsome on a man, the same features appeared very odd indeed under one of Aunt Mary's shabbily haphazard bonnets.

"Is it the dispensary that makes the bazaar special?" asked William shyly. "Or is it something else?"

"Goodness!" exclaimed Aunt Mary. "I've forgotten to tell you! No. It's little Miss Veena Basu. She is coming to England next summer and has promised to come down to Rushby and speak at our bazaar."

"Veena Basu. Veena Basu . . ." repeated Ellen, racking her brains to remember where she had heard the name before.

"I remember!" said Rob, jumping about in his chair. "She's the one who came to Christ at the Easter picnic by the Taralpur Canal."

"Yes, Rob," said Aunt Mary, sounding somewhat startled. "If that's the way you like to put it."

It was not Rob who put it that way, thought Ellen. It was the missionary magazine.

"What is Miss Basu doing in England?" asked William.

"It is a wonderful story really," answered Aunt Mary eagerly. "You remember that she has been helping Miss Drury in the dispensary?"

They nodded their heads. They remembered now.

"Well, her father has been so impressed by Miss Drury's work in the zenanas—and by the change in his daughter—that he has become a Christian, too. And, since he is a very rich man and has a brother here in England in the tea trade, he is taking the very unusual step of sending his daughter to this country so that she can receive a sound medical training."

"So she'll really be here in Rushby in September?" asked Ellen excitedly. "I've never seen an Indian girl before."

"It's nothing," said Rob, suddenly scornful. "I've got an Indian boy in my form at St. Olaves. He's just like us—except he sort of singsongs when he talks—and he's brown."

"Yes. But an Indian *girl* in Rushby!"

Ellen could not get over the wonder.

"Don't you think Venna Basu's coming makes it a very special bazaar?" said Aunt Mary, smiling happily.

Yes, they agreed. It made it very special indeed.

"Her coming will bring in the County from far and wide," said Ellen. "Everyone will want to see an Indian girl."

"And they'll all spend a lot of money at the stalls," said Rob.

"So Miss Drury will get her dispensary in no time," grinned William.

"Yes," concluded their aunt with amused satisfaction.

Unworldly though she was, no one had a smarter eye for the main chance when it came to raising funds for the Zenana Mission.

Though it was only January and the bazaar was still eight

months ahead, Aunt Mary began there and then to deploy her forces. William and Rob, she said, were to busy themselves in their school carpentry lessons in making stools, trays, and frames for fire screens.

"And you, Ellen, will draw designs for the screens, and Martha Paddle will work them in Berlin wool."

Martha Paddle was a member of the Rushby Girls' Bible Class which met at seven o'clock every Saturday morning in Aunt Mary's drawing room. Ellen was a member, too. While Aunt Mary expounded the scriptures, the girls sewed pinafores and babies' clothes and embroidered articles for the bazaar— a happy marriage of intellectual and practical Christianity which brought the greatest satisfaction to all concerned, for the Bible Class began with breakfast and, as Ellen had to admit, Aunt Mary's cook made the creamiest porridge ever known in Rushby. Better still, no one counted how many spoonfuls of sugar one took.

"And your dear mother," continued Aunt Mary, "must knit dozens of pairs of those stockings of hers."

Knitting was their mother's great claim to fame in the matter of the bazaar. She knitted beautifully. She had learned the art at the age of six in knitting wristlets for Miss Nightingale's soldiers in the Crimean War.

"And what are *you* going to make?" Rob asked his aunt.

Aunt Mary was the best wood-carver for miles around; some of her work was to be seen in the village churches. Her beautiful set of tools was the only possession of hers which she refused to allow Rob to borrow.

"I am carving a panel representing the raising of Lazarus for St. Felix church at Mutby," she explained. "And in return, Mr. Fellows has promised to drive a wagonload of his parishioners over for the bazaar."

"So we must have hundreds and hundreds of things for them to buy," said William.

"And a Punch and Judy Show," urged Ellen. "Please let's have Punch and Judy again."

"And the ice-cream man," demanded Rob. "And Mr. Brooks with his tricks."

"Goodness, but of course!" exclaimed Aunt Mary. "And much else, besides. I had thought of bowling for a pig on Uncle Martin's top lawn and the Volunteer Band playing under the apple trees around the pond."

"Do you think we could run three-legged races and things?" suggested Rob.

"And archery?"

"And a sweet stall with toffee apples and coconut ice?" asked Ellen, whose mind those days always seemed to be dwelling on food.

"We must have everything. Everything," said Aunt Mary happily. "With little Miss Veena Basu coming to us all the way from Taralpur, we must make it the most splendid bazaar that Rushby has ever known."

≥ 2 ≤

By the end of the first week in the following September, Rushby was at the height of its annual attack of "bazaar fever." What if it rained on the great day? What if it was too hot and melted Signor Manuello's ice cornets? What if nobody turned up? What—on the other hand—if so many people came that there were not enough of Wyatt's sugar buns to go around? The anxieties of the grown-ups were of a more complex and acrimonious nature. Mrs. Thwaite was offended that Miss Lark had been put in charge of the fancy stall, and the Rector was angry with Aunt Mary for having invited the Mayor.

"But we always invite the Mayor," their aunt explained to their mother.

"Surely not when the Mayor is a Methodist, Mary? Besides, Mr. Fitt is such a vulgar little man. He has not an 'h' to his name."

How could he have, thought Ellen, seeing that Mr. Fitt's Christian names were Alfred Septimus Bert?

But she knew that it was not her mother's lack of logic that caused her aunt to frown.

"Mr. Fitt is a *good* man, Cara," Aunt Mary said severely, and then relented and smiled as she added: "Besides, he always sends us six casks of ginger beer for the Volunteer Band."

Ellen blushed and prayed that the matter would be left at that, for her mother had been known to remark that there was no one so wily as a Methodist grocer in advertising his trade.

But her mother contented herself with hoping that the upstart Mayor would not embarrass them all by thinking that he was entitled to hob nob with the County, and then passed on to other things. Who, for example, was to meet Miss Veena Basu at the railway station?

"The Rector and his wife have agreed to do that," explained Aunt Mary. "Uncle Martin and Samantha are kindly lending us their carriage. Simkins will set the three of them down at the garden gate."

Great-Uncle Martin and frail old cousin Samantha!

It was these two antiquities, Ellen always thought, who really bore the brunt of the Zenana Mission Bazaar—for, from time immemorial, this great event had been held in Great-

Uncle Martin's immense, rambling, and overgrown garden. "I don't know. I don't know at all," the old man would begin muttering every year as he watched the men putting up the tea tent on the croquet lawn. "I don't know. I really don't know."

"Which is very odd of him," William remarked, seeing that Great-Uncle Martin had once been a Cambridge professor and known all that there was to know about anything one would care to name.

"Well, he *is* ninety-one," Ellen retorted. "And it *is* the bazaar."

His daughter, poor cousin Samantha, went around wringing her hands.

"I do hope, my dears, that the Volunteers will not trample down the red-hot pokers."

But it was Great-Uncle Martin's gardener who was most put out by the whole affair.

"Pickin' me lovely grapes?" he grumbled indignantly as he stood on a ladder in the greenhouse wielding a pair of scissors. "Pickin' me lovely grapes for the sake of a set o' naked heathens?"

"They're *not* heathens. They're Christians," Rob shouted up at him rudely. "And if you were out in India in all that heat, you'd probably go around with nothing on, too, Mr. Barber."

In short, everyone except Aunt Mary was in a considerable fuss.

It was early in the morning on the Wednesday before the Saturday of the Bazaar that Ellen walked down to her Aunt Mary's house to help sort the jumble.

"Drat those Bibles," she exclaimed irritably as she stumbled over the stacks of holy books piled up on the front-door step.

She had forgotten that it was market day. Aunt Mary always put out Bibles on market day, just in case one of the farmers or drovers or gipsies who came into Rushby on Wednesdays should be called by the Lord and feel in need of His Holy Word. It was a matter of "Help yourself."

"And no one ever has," Ellen thought crossly as she retrieved the books sprawled across the pavement. "Or ever will."

Two hours later, she recalled her bad temper in horror, wondering superstitiously whether her dratting of the Bible had brought down the wrath of God upon Aunt Mary's bazaar.

They were tossing the jumble of articles for the rummage table about at the time. William was methodically picking out the clothes which were too dirty to sell and taking them off to the bonfire in Aunt Mary's garden. And Rob was fooling about in his usual way.

"What's this?" he asked, grinning, holding up a pair of pink whaleboned corsets with black laces.

"Put it down," snapped Ellen. "It's not the sort of garment you ought to know about."

And they returned to the sensual fingering of blue cashmeres, sealskin, and crimson plush, and held up long, trailing boas, and mantles glittering with thousands of little beads. It was a feast of color and feel.

"Oh, Ellen!" cried Rob a minute later in ecstatic joy. "Look at this. Look at this!"

From under a pile of thick dolmans and mantlets, he pulled out yards and yards of beautiful green silk.

"What ever is it?" she asked in wonder, staring down at the verdant river of silk meandering over the table. "A curtain, do you think?"

Rob snatched it up and swathed it around his body.

"How wonderful to be a girl!" he exclaimed. "And to be able to wear a color like this!"

It was a pity it was faded all across the top and had a large scorch mark in the middle, she thought. One could have made it up into a beautiful summer dress.

"Dears; oh, my dears," said Aunt Mary softly.

They turned around in surprise to find their aunt standing in the doorway, white in the face, with a letter in her hand.

"What's the matter, Aunt Mary?" asked William, coming in from the garden.

Aunt Mary sat down on a chair, clearly much shaken.

"Oh, my dears, poor little Veena Basu is ill. She cannot come."

"Can't *come!*" exclaimed Ellen. "How awful! What about the bazaar?"

Aunt Mary recovered from her weakness.

"It is the poor child's illness we should think about," she said. "Not the bazaar."

"What's the letter say?" asked Rob.

Aunt Mary handed it to William.

"You read it to them," she said.

William frowned at the unusual writing, then cleared his throat and read the following:

Honourable Lady,

It is with grief I write you my daughter Veena is sudden ill. She has great pain so that we take her, my brother and I, into the Ladies' Hospital. Miss Doctor say Veena must have treatment. An operation. I do not know. Veena is very sad not come to Rushby. She beg you forgive the trouble.

I am, yours highly obliged,
Buta Basu.

"What ever's the matter with her?" asked Ellen. "It sounds so odd to have been taken ill so suddenly."

"Perhaps it is that new disease your father was talking about," murmured Aunt Mary.

"Appendicitis," said William.

The three of them stared down wretchedly at their disappointed aunt and then scowled at the tawdry piles of hateful rummage.

"It's spoiled the whole thing," said Rob in disgust, kicking

78

angrily into a stack of men's shoes. "Not half the number of people will turn up—and we shan't get the £400."

"Don't let's tell anyone she's not coming," Ellen was surprised to hear herself suggest.

Aunt Mary's moral reproofs had a way of working through silence.

One could have heard a pin drop.

"Ellen," she said quietly, at last. "That is not honest. I shall write to the Rector and Lady Tarrington at once."

Yet all was not lost.

On the Friday afternoon, while Tom Taylor, the carpenter, was hammering together the stand for the Volunteer Band and Ellen and her friend, Rowena Bayly, were setting out the chairs for the Committee, William came leaping over Cousin Samantha's pansy bed, shouting at the top of his voice:

"It's all right, Ellen. It's all right. She's coming, after all."

"Veena Basu?" she asked, hardly believing her ears.

Aunt Mary had just received a telegram, he gabbled. Miss Basu was quite recovered. She was out of the hospital and would be arriving at Rushby tomorrow by the train that had been arranged.

"It must have been green gooseberries, or something," he grinned. "Not appendicitis, after all."

Ellen could hardly contain her joy. She flung her arms around Rowena and would have flung them around William, too, if Rowena had not been there.

"But how are we going to let everyone know?" she asked excitedly.

William grinned again.

"Trust Aunt Mary," he replied. "She's hired the town crier. Listen!"

Tom Taylor had stopped his hammering, and the four of them stood listening in Great-Uncle Martin's, bird-chattering, bee-humming garden to the ringing of the town crier's bell.

"Oyez! Oyez!" came his cry from the top of Blyburgate. "Tomorrow Miss Veena Basu from India . . ."

That evening, her heart overflowing with happiness, Ellen stood in the churchyard, gazing west over the Norfolk marshes at the most glorious sunset she could ever remember. Great golden towers and valleys of fire stood in the sky behind Gillingham village.

"Red sky at night
A shepherd's delight,"

she murmured happily to herself. Tomorrow was going to be fine.

≥ 3 ≤

The great day dawned so bright and fair that by breakfast time the sun was shining out of a dazzling azure sky.

"I'm going to see an Indian girl. An Indian girl. An Indian girl," Ellen chanted inside her head as she buttered her second slice of bread.

She was so excited that she did not know how she was going to get through the long morning. She and Rowena, she decided at last, would go down to Great-Uncle Martin's garden and walk up and down the long gravel paths with their arms knotted together behind their backs and watch the ladies arranging their stalls. With luck, they would be able to slip into the raspberry canes and eat the last of the white raspberries. That was what they would do.

"Ellen, I want you to stay quietly at home this morning," broke in her mother—just as though she had been eavesdropping on her thoughts.

"Why?"

"There's a long day ahead. And you look peaked."

"I'm all right," she protested rebelliously. "I'm perfectly all right."

"You will do as I say, all the same," replied her mother with finality. "I want you to look your best. Lady Tarrington will be bringing Charmian and Sophia over this afternoon. It would be nice if you could make friends."

Ellen groaned. Her father had already left the room, so there was no one to restrain her mother's grandiose flights of fancy. The Tarringtons were rich. They were well-born. They possessed the finest house in the whole of south Norfolk. And in two or three years they would be giving balls for their twin daughters. Ellen knew it all. Every word of it. She knew Charmian and Sophia, too; and disliked them as much as they disliked her. Their mutual misliking was so intense that it could never be cured by a mere mother.

"What are the boys going to do this morning?" Ellen asked spitefully.

"I've got messages to run for Aunt Mary," Rob replied hurriedly. "I'll probably stay and have lunch with her—so don't worry if I'm not back."

"And William?"

William was going to catch up on the Latin that had been set for his holiday task, he said.

Ellen retired to the schoolroom in a sulk and tried to forget herself in *Ivanhoe*. But she felt far too frustrated and excited and kept looking out of the window to see if the wagonloads of people had begun arriving from the country.

"I don't think this afternoon is ever going to come," she sighed peevishly as she watched the minute hand shudder its way to eleven o'clock.

But it did.

It came ravishingly at half past one to the strains of the Volunteer Band playing "Soldiers of the Queen" as it marched across the Market Square.

"Come, Mother. It's time we were off," shouted Ellen, tearing down the stairs.

As mother and daughter walked seemingly sedately down Blyburgate behind the soldiers, Mrs. Henchman suddenly said:

"Bless the Volunteers! Do you know, Ellen, when your father first brought me to Rushby as a bride, the Volunteers met us at the station? They unharnessed the horses; they got between the shafts; and they pulled the carriage all the way up Station Road!"

"Did they really," said Ellen with cruel absentmindedness. The band had just broken into "Onward Christian Soldiers," and she was being swept up on the crest of a huge, swelling wave of pride and joy.

"How wonderful to be English!" she thought. "How glorious to be C. of E.!"

Great-Uncle Martin's garden was already dotted with ladies clad in leg-of-mutton–sleeved blouses and huge bell skirts, all daintily twirling their parasols. With the music and the color and the laughter, it was just like a ball.

"We are not waiting for Miss Basu, Cara," said Aunt Mary as she greeted them. "We are opening the stalls straight away."

Ellen escaped to find Rowena standing by the clump of bamboos, throwing phlox petals into the pond.

"Come along, Rowena," she said. "Let's go and buy the best of the coconut ice, while it's still to be had."

More and more people were streaming into the garden. Lord Tarrington's carriage had just arrived—and Mr. Miles Grange's from Sotterley. The great landowners and their families were now jostling around the stalls with the humbler parishioners of Rushby.

"Come and buy. Come and buy." Aunt Mary beamed on all within range. "We are not waiting for Miss Basu. Her train does not arrive until after three."

There was suddenly a great deal of shouting and vulgar guffawing on the upper lawn.

"What's happened?" asked Ellen of a flustered-looking William, running past.

"They're bowling for a pig," he gasped.

"But why all the noise?"

"The pig escaped into the asparagus bed. I've just pulled it out."

"Look!" exclaimed Rowena with a giggle. "The wagon must have arrived from Mutby."

Great-Uncle Martin's garden was suddenly bobbing with bonnets and bright print dresses and murmurous with the soft drawl of Suffolk country voices.

"Come and buy. Come and buy," said Aunt Mary. "It will soon be time for the speeches."

Half an hour later, almost penniless of pocket and very thirsty for tea and lemonade, the company assembled on the wide lawn fronting the green-mantled lily pond.

"Now sit yourselves down," said Aunt Mary in her most

comfortable voice. "Grown-ups on the chairs, of course. Children on the rugs."

She had a great sense of occasion. Miss Veena Basu was her trump card—and the card, so to speak, had to be played with a thump.

"Our President, Lady Tarrington, will talk to us all for a few minutes," she continued, smiling. "Then we shall all sing a hymn. And then . . . and then it will be time for . . . for who do you think?"

"For Miss Basu," chorused the Rushby Girls' Bible Class entirely unprompted.

"For Miss Basu," Aunt Mary agreed, nodding at Lady Tarrington as a sign that she should begin her piece.

Lady Tarrington rambled on at such length she would have spoiled the whole, carefully-designed effect, had not Aunt Mary very pointedly unpinned the gold watch fastened to her dress and looked at it exceedingly closely. Then the poor president sat down, and the band began playing through the tune for the hymn.

"Oh, good!" whispered Ellen. "It's *'Greenland's icy mountains.'*"

They were sitting somewhat haphazardly on a green tartan rug—Rowena, Ellen, William, and the horrible Augustus Peebles—on the very edge of the pond.

Out came the first verse in a healthy, happy roar. And then away they went with the second.

> *"What though the spicy breezes*
> *Blow soft o'er Ceylon's isle?"*

they sang. And—as if in heaven-sent answer—Miss Veena Basu, clad in emerald *sari,* her head charmingly draped in white gold cloth, walked delicately down the garden path between the Rector and his wife.

"Oh . . . ," breathed Ellen ecstatically, leaving Bishop Heber's great mission hymn to take care of itself, "she's beautiful! Absolutely beautiful!"

Miss Veena Basu was slim and straight and rather short. She walked with the little tripping steps necessary for one who wears a *sari,* and as she turned, now to left, now to right, her teeth flashed white in her dusky face. The engaging friendliness of her smile bewitched everyone in the garden.

> *"The heathen in his blindness"*

faltered the Rushby Girl's Bible Class, and nearly came to a stop.

"She's charming!" "She's so little!" people murmured.

To think that anyone so young and fragile was actually going to be a doctor, William marveled as he watched the girl from India mount the stage and modestly take her place between two members of the Committee.

"Salvation! oh, salvation!"

roared the men's choir, determined to keep their astonishment till later.

And now, Lady Tarrington was extending her hymn book and the marvelous girl was singing, too.

> *"Waft, waft, ye winds, His story,*
> *And you, ye waters, roll,"*

came the triumphant roar from everyone assembled in Great-Uncle Martin's garden.

"What a day! What a wonderful day!" thought Ellen, completely carried away by Miss Basu and her own intense missionary fervor.

"She's got *blue* eyes," said Augustus Peebles indignantly when the hymn came to an end and they were all settling themselves more comfortably on the rug, waiting for Aunt Mary to address them.

"Well, she comes from one of those northern tribes, that's why," said Rowena sharply. "Lots of them have blue eyes up in the mountains—and red hair, too, I believe."

Ellen looked at her friend with new respect. Rowena was always surprising one with her odd bits of knowledge.

"Dear people," began Aunt Mary. "Dear friends of the Mission, we have, today, the great honor and happiness of welcoming a new young Christian from Taralpur itself. Miss

Basu is a keen worker in the zenanas and a valued helpmate of our good Miss Drury. . . ."

Aunt Mary spoke briefly and well. Miss Basu, she said, was in London to train as a doctor. She had undertaken the long train journey down to Rushby today with great sacrifice to herself, for she had not been well. What was more, she was here for only a brief hour, for it was imperative for her to return to London on the 4:15 train.

"She has kindly consented to tell us a little about her life in India and about the work of our Mission," she said in conclusion. "But, remember, English is not Miss Basu's native tongue, so her little talk must, of necessity, be very brief."

Everyone clapped loudly as Aunt Mary turned to Miss Basu and tenderly presented her to her audience.

The young Indian girl looked suddenly rather nervous. Ellen felt anxious for her.

"If she wasn't so terribly brown, I expect she'd be blushing like a poppy," passed through her head.

"De-arr lediz an shentlemen," began Miss Basu.

She spoke rapidly in a singsong voice—just like Rob's schoolfriend—so that it was not always easy to understand what she said, and she stopped, engagingly, every now and then, to seek for the right word. It was very wicked of her countrymen, she told them, to keep their wives and daughters shut up in the zenanas. The women were idle and ignorant and greedy.

"What if I say to you they do nothing but eat sweetmeats?" asked Miss Veena Basu, her white teeth flashing in a smile. "And play wi'd their pet birds?"

Ellen felt an uncomfortable little worm of a thought turning in her brain.

But Miss Basu had left the subject of the zenanas, apparently, for words like "jungle," "pythons," "tigers," suddenly appeared in her singsong tale.

"Sometimes," she confessed, "in de tent at night wi'd Miss Drury, I hear de scream of parakeets and de roar of lions."

Lions!

Ellen let out a gasp. She suddenly felt very ill indeed.

"Lions!" whispered Rowena incredulously. "But you don't find lions in *India!*"

To show the size of the lions, Miss Basu had stretched out her arms, like a fisherman boasting of his catch.

"Good God!" exclaimed the startled Augustus.

Ellen followed his gaze in panic.

From under the many folds of the emerald *sari* had appeared a large scorch mark in the shape of a flatiron.

"It's our old drawing-room curtain," muttered Augustus, not yet fully believing his eyes.

Ellen looked wildly at William.

"It's Rob," she whispered.

And then, since William did not seem to understand, she gave him a sharp dig with her elbow.

"Miss Basu is *Rob*," she hissed, frantic with fear.

Augustus was trying to struggle to his feet.

"Stop him, William," she said hoarsely. "You must stop him."

William was no fool. His mind worked like a bomb. He suddenly grappled the enemy in such a fierce tackle that both he and Augustus somersaulted backwards with a resounding splash into Great-Uncle Martin's green-mantled lily pond.

"Dear Lord. Dear Lord," Ellen found herself praying. "Please ring down the curtain. Please, *please* send a thunderbolt or an eclipse . . . or . . . or the ten plagues of Egypt."

Miss Basu had stopped speaking. Everyone had turned around and was gaping at the pond.

Alas! The Lord did not oblige.

Very slowly, covered with duckweed, the two boys' heads emerged.

"That's not Miss Basu," Augustus spluttered out in rage. "It's Rob Henchman."

Rob Henchman!

With sinking heart, Ellen saw the entire bazaar turn angrily towards the rostrum.

Rob was no fool, either. He picked up his *sari* and was dashing off, barelegged and sandal-footed, in the direction of the raspberry canes.

≫ 4 ≪

"How could you *do* such a thing?" thundered their father at the three of them.

Their mother felt so ill that she had retired to bed.

"How could you do such a *dreadful* thing to your Aunt Mary?"

"It wasn't the others," choked Rob.

Rob looked utterly miserable under the glistening blackness of the burnt cork.

"You have disgraced yourselves," roared their father, unheeding. "And you have disgraced the best and kindest woman you know."

"But . . . but," faltered a white-faced William, "they won't think *she* knew anything about it, will they?"

"Oh, no, Father," said Ellen, bursting into tears. "Not Aunt Mary. They *couldn't!*"

Their father considered the point a little more calmly.

"No," he admitted at last. "They cannot. Rushby has known your aunt for fifty years. The town has never had a more upright or honorable citizen."

He turned his back on them all, moved by his sister's goodness and by his own children's disgrace.

"But the same cannot be said of you," he swung back at them, his face gray and lined by the disastrous events of the day.

In the dusk, the three of them trailed miserably down to Aunt Mary's house. Ellen had tried to scrub the burnt cork off Rob's face and hands but had only succeeded in making them red and sore; they were still streaked with brown.

The poor boy looked ill with wretchedness.

"I only did it to help," he gulped. "I thought it'd get Miss Drury that dispensary she wants."

"But Rob . . ."

What was there to say?

As they stood on the front-door steps, William nervously tapped the knocker.

"What do you want?" asked Emily, the parlormaid, peering at them in the shadows.

She sounded very cross.

"To see Aunt Mary," said William.

"I'm not sure she wants to see *you*," came Emily's tart reply. "Your aunt's tired. She wants to go to bed."

"Who is it, Emily?" came Aunt Mary's voice from the stairs.

"Master William, Mum. And Miss Ellen and Master Robert. Shall I tell them to go away?"

"No. Tell them to come in."

Her voice did indeed sound very tired—and sad.

They stood in a row in the hall while their aunt looked down upon them from halfway up the stairs. She had a lighted candle in her right hand and *The Church Times* tucked under her left arm.

"Well?" she asked.

"I'm so sorry, Aunt Mary," burst out the unhappy Rob. "I really am."

She gazed down compassionately at her nephew's piteously piebald face.

"I am sure you are, Rob," she said sadly.

Then she turned to William and Ellen.

"Were you in the deception, too?" she asked.

Slowly they shook their heads.

"Well, Rob," she sighed as she continued her journey upstairs. "I suppose you did your best."

They watched her poor bent back as she went up to bed, each hurt almost past bearing that the unlucky Rob had given her such pain.

"She's so upset," thought Ellen, "that it's killed all her tenderness and fun."

But she was wrong.

"Ellen," said her aunt with her back to them. "Try a little vaseline on Rob's face. It is kinder than the scrubbing brush."

"Yes, Aunt Mary."

At the turn of the stairs, she paused and looked down at them once more, a faint smile hovering over her lips.

"The Rector and I have counted the takings," she said, the smile growing a good deal more certain.

"What have we got?" asked Ellen.

"Four hundred and three pounds, ten shillings, and two buttons."

Rob's poor face cracked into a grin.

"So she's got her dispensary after all!"

Aunt Mary nodded her head. Her smile was now as broad and forgiving as the sun.

"Now, good night to you all," she said. "I am off to bed."

The Explosion

Just after Christmas, Dr. Jameson and his six hundred troopers raided the Transvaal and set the whole world by the ears.

"It's disgraceful!" Aunt Mary exclaimed, as she hurried into the morning room with the newspaper open in her hand. "Unprovoked aggression! We ought to be ashamed of ourselves!"

"Nonsense, Mary," Mrs. Henchman replied sharply. "The Boers deserve everything they may get. They have no right to stand in the way of progress."

"*Progress,* Cara? Our greed for gold can hardly be called progress."

Ellen looked from her aunt to her mother and sighed. She wished they would agree about something for once. It was disturbing when grown-ups were at odds. Then she shrugged her shoulders. South Africa was a long way off, and she and William and Rob had matters of far greater moment to attend to, quite close at hand.

First, there was the Suffolk bomb scare; secondly, Colonel Petrie's arrival in Rushby; and lastly—and most exciting of all—the Colonel's splendid suggestion that they should all act a play.

The mystery of the bomb scare, it is true, had already been solved. Just before Christmas an unhappy young man had been charged with arson.

"He's clearly not right in the head," William had explained to Rob and herself. "For who in his senses would want to blow up such an extraordinary lot of things as Mr. Dunnage's potato clamp, the Bellingham family tomb, and the Ladies' Underwear Department at the Eastwold Working Men's Stores?"

"Perhaps he just liked the fun of it," Rob had suggested.

But fun or no fun, the affair was now closed. And if the young man and his bombs lived on in people's minds, this was only to be noticed in the sudden interest in explosives evinced by every schoolboy in the town and by a tendency in all parents to jump a foot in the air at any unexpected bang.

Colonel Petrie and his play were far more important. Ellen and Rob could think of little else, for no child in Rushby had ever acted in a proper play before. Indeed, until their new friend's arrival, Ellen suspected that play acting might even have been considered sinful or—at best—a woeful waste of time.

"Play acting!" exclaimed the Colonel. "Why, it's the greatest fun in the world!"

And because the new arrival was clearly both a gentleman and a Christian and—moreover—a widower with a daughter of his own, all the mamas of Rushby suddenly agreed that amateur theatricals were the very thing. Why had they never thought of them before?

"I always find the Christmas holidays a great cross," Ellen heard Mrs. Peebles confide to her mother.

"Yes, a play will give them something to do."

"And keep them out of the house."

"And out of mischief, too."

They were all sitting comfortably on the drawing-room floor at Montagu House. Chestnuts were roasting in the grate.

"Well, what is our play to be?" asked Colonel Petrie of his guests.

He barked out his remarks like an amiable dog.

"Something by Shakespeare, sir," suggested Augustus.

"No," shouted Rob in disgust. "Shakespeare's for school. Not the holidays."

"What about a sort of pantomine . . . ?" volunteered Rowena.

It was a sensible idea, for most of the children were very young—far younger than Rowena and William and Ellen, even younger than Rob and Augustus.

Ellen looked at the bright eyes and shy faces of the seven- and eight-year-olds, warm in the firelight, and thought of field mice.

"Yes, *Cinderella* or *Babes in the Wood*," she suggested.

"*Babes in the Wood*," jeered Rob. "We're not *babies*. I thought we were going to act a proper play."

William had said nothing all this time, which was not surprising for he quite often said nothing. But, on turning to him, Ellen saw that on this occasion there was a special reason for his silence. He was gazing wonder-struck at Felicia Petrie.

Felicia was twelve years old. She was straight-haired, gray-eyed, thoughtful, and lovely. "And she does not know that she is any of these things," thought Ellen, gazing at her, too. "She is quite unconscious of how charming she is."

William suddenly stopped staring at her and addressed his host.

"I think that our play should be *Alice in Wonderland,* sir," he said.

Rowena gave the matter her lightning thought.

"Yes, *Alice,*" she exclaimed with enthusiasm. "Do let's act *Alice.* It's just the thing. There are parts for all of us . . . old and young. And it's not too serious. And it isn't silly, either."

"But it's a book, sir, not a play," objected Augustus with the heavy accuracy of the scholar.

"Daddy is very good at turning things into plays," said Felicia quietly. "Will you do it for us, Daddy?"

The Colonel looked down upon his oddly assorted cast.

"Of course, if it is the play that you would really like us to do."

"Yes. Yes," squeaked the field mice. "Do let's act *Alice.*"

Only Rob was dumb. Ellen grinned at his dumbness, for she knew that he had refused to read *Alice* in the nursery "because it was all about a silly girl."

The Colonel strode to the library bookshelf and pulled down the two *Alice* books. And, in the end, it was decided that he should write a series of sketches drawn from both *Alice in Wonderland* and *Through the Looking Glass.*

"It looks quite easy to do," he smiled as his eyes glanced down the pages. "The books are almost a play already."

Then, after roast chestnuts and toasted marshmallows, he

sent Rob and Augustus and the younger children home and settled down to the serious business of casting with William and Ellen and Rowena.

"Another year, I shall know you all better," he explained, "and shall be able to cast the Christmas play myself. But this year you will have to help me."

"How?" asked Rowena.

"Tell me what you are all like."

The three of them looked inwards upon themselves and wondered anxiously how much they would have to tell.

"We . . . we've never acted in a play before, sir," blurted out William. "I don't really know what any of us will be like on a stage."

The Colonel was a patient man—in spite of being a colonel.

"Well, let's start at the beginning," he smiled, turning to the two girls. "Which of you would like to be Alice?"

"Not me," said Rowena quickly. "I'm too old."

Ellen was filled with panic, for at the thought of taking the principal part, she suddenly felt stiff and awkward—like an ill-jointed puppet.

"Nor me," she gasped. "I'm much too tall."

"But, sir!" exclaimed William in surprise. "Felicia is to be Alice. I thought that it was all settled."

"By whom?" asked a cool, precise voice from the hearth-rug.

Felicia had turned back from the glowing coals and was looking at them inquiringly, a marshmallow speared on a knitting needle, poised in her hand.

They gazed back at her, all four of them. The firelight shone in her long, fair hair and played over her grave, intelligent face.

"By whom?" she asked again.

They laughed.

Alice Liddell had fallen down a Rushby chimney and, with her usual composure, had dusted herself down and taken to toasting marshmallows.

"It's a unanimous decision, my dear," said her father.

"Tweedledum!" exclaimed Rob in alarm. "What sort of an animal is that?"

What with Rowena taking the part of a walrus and Ellen a mock turtle, and William saying that he had agreed to be a caterpillar—a caterpillar that smoked a hookah, of all things— Rob hated to think what sort of creature the others had landed him with.

"He's a fat little man," laughed Ellen.

"Who looks like an egg in an eggcup," explained Rowena.

"But *I'm* not fat," protested Rob angrily.

"We'll pad you with a cushion," laughed William.

"It's not fair," he continued to grumble indignantly. "Not even with a cushion in my middle could I look like an egg in an eggcup. Why didn't you make me a rabbit or a hamster or a dog? I'm sure there must be one decent kind of animal in the silly book."

"Why," laughed Rowena, "you had to be Tweedledum because of Tweedledee."

"Tweedledee? What's that?"

"Your twin," shrieked Ellen, flinging herself on the schoolroom settee and burying her face in a cushion.

"What—*another* little fat man?"

Rowena nodded her head, speechless with laughter. The joke had clearly not come to an end.

"And who's taking the part of Tweedledee?" demanded Rob angrily.

The three of them looked at him in silence—suddenly doubtful.

"Augustus Peebles," said William.

Rob roared like the bulls of Bashan.

"*Not* Augustus! I won't be his twin! I won't. I won't."

"But listen, Rob," Rowena tried to explain.

Rob would not listen.

"I won't act in your silly play—not . . . not if I've got to be twin to that loathsome lump of lard."

"*Listen,* you fool," shouted William.

"Don't you see," said Rowena quickly. "The twins . . . they're always quarrelling."

"Oh," said Rob, slightly mollified.

"Whenever one of them says 'Nohow,' the other contradicts and shouts 'Contrariwise.' "

"Well, I suppose that's not quite so bad," he conceded ungraciously.

"And then . . . then, at the end," babbled Ellen. "They have a duel. They wear coal scuttles on their heads for helmets."

"Sounds pretty silly to me," said Rob.

The others sighed with relief, for despite his scorn, they could see he was won over. The light of battle gleamed in his eyes. Clearly the chance of a fight with Augustus—a fight actually sanctioned by a grown-up and to be fought on a stage in front of the whole town—was a joy not to be missed.

"Where shall we get the coal scuttles from?" he asked suddenly, grinning eagerly. "And what did they fight with? Pistols? Rapiers?"

"A sword," said Ellen somewhat uneasily.

"And who won?"

He had forgotten the most important point of all.

William looked down his nose in perplexity.

"It was a . . . a kind of draw," said Rowena in haste.

Not one of them dared to tell him that Tweedledum and Tweedledee were such arrant cowards that they never actually *fought* the duel.

"Oh dear, oh dear," Ellen groaned afterwards, on looking back on the whole affair. "How right Father was when he told us never to tell a lie!"

"Well, it wasn't exactly a lie," sighed Rowena. "Tweedledum and Tweedledee *did* quarrel; they *did* set out to have a duel; and they *did* wear coal scuttles on their heads."

"Yes, but we deceived Rob. You know we did."

And—as everyone knew—their deception had led to the most appallingly explosive results.

Next day the parts were handed out, and everyone settled down to work in an atmosphere of pleased excitement. Ellen was overjoyed at being allowed to paint the scenery.

"Use as much paint and make as much mess as you like," barked the Colonel.

William, whose part as the Caterpillar was hardly onerous, made himself responsible for the props and the stage carpentry; while Rowena and a number of the mothers undertook to make the costumes. Rob, being Rob, gave everyone else advice about their tasks and forgot to learn more than the first page of Tweedledum's part.

But at the first rehearsal there was trouble, for Felicia Petrie proved even more enchanting on the stage than off it, and Rob and Augustus, who had scarcely noticed her before, both suddenly fell desperately in love with her—at least, that is what Ellen suspected. Augustus kept offering her bull's-eyes out of a sticky bag, and Rob was furiously incensed when he discovered that Tweedledee had the honor of reciting the whole of the poem of "The Walrus and the Carpenter" to Alice while poor Tweedledum stood on the stage saying nothing at all.

"It's not fair, sir," he told the Colonel roundly. "I think we ought to say one verse each."

Since Augustus was reciting the verses with the solemnity of a Hamlet, the Colonel quickly agreed.

"Yes, Robert, I think you have a point there. Augustus, you can take the first verse and Robert the second . . . and so on.

And then Rowena, you come in as the Walrus, and James as the Carpenter."

Ellen sighed with relief, for Rob might now feel less cheated when he discovered that the duel was never to take place. Everyone was still reading his part from his script—and Rob, of course, had not glanced at the end of the scene.

But it was a forlorn hope.

Rob was bitterly disappointed.

"I thought we were going to have a *proper* fight," he exclaimed in disgust. "Not run away. What's more, I *won't* run away. I'm not afraid of Augustus."

"You're in a play, you silly," hissed Rowena from the wings. "You're Tweedledum, not yourself."

"Besides, Robert," explained the patient producer. "The twins are really quite fond of each other underneath. When they first appear on the stage, we've got to have them embracing."

"Embracing? Me embrace Augustus," Rob roared in outrage. "I'd rather blow up a bank."

Ellen gasped. Rob was impossible. But Felicia, new to his ways, was so startled by his insult that she burst out laughing. Taunted and mocked, Augustus hurled himself at Rob's middle with a snarl of rage, and the two of them rolled over and over across the floor.

When William and the Colonel had separated them and shaken them like two puppies, the Colonel issued an ultimatum.

"Robert, if you wish to remain in the play, you must make friends with Augustus AT ONCE. If not, I shall waste no more time with you."

Rob looked miserable and embarrassed and rebellious all at

the same moment. Augustus was still white to the eyes with rage.

"Now, shake hands both of you."

Rob raised his head like an unhappy mule.

"Please, please, Rob," said Felicia.

He put out his hand.

"Well, that might have been worse," said Ellen to Rowena as they walked home up Northgate after the next rehearsal.

"Worse?" laughed Rowena. "I thought it was wonderful. Rob was a joy."

Rob had, in fact, excelled himself, for once he had got it into his thick head that on stage he was Tweedledum and nobody else, he had thrown himself into the part with verve. For all his superior intelligence and fine diction, poor Augustus had seemed a very pale shadow in his wake.

"I'm so glad," sighed Ellen happily, "so glad he isn't going to spoil all the fun."

For fun, it certainly was. She could never remember such a happy Christmas holiday before. There were suddenly so many things to do; so many things to talk and laugh about. Besides, though she could not confess it even to Rowena, the rehearsal they had just left had brought a small triumph to Ellen, too.

"Why, my dear, that's splendid! What a gifted child you are!" the Colonel had exclaimed upon seeing her first attempt at stage scenery.

There were very few compliments to be picked up at home at this time, for her mother was clearly disappointed with her for being so clumsy and awkward. "Ellen, sit up straight," she kept nagging. Or, "Quietly, quietly, child. Try to remember you are not a young horse." She had to walk twice around the drawing room every morning, balancing an atlas on her head, with her mother exclaiming: "Smile, Ellen. Don't frown."

"It's as though she's training me for a circus act," she would grumble wretchedly to herself.

And so, when Colonel Petrie praised her painting, something precious and very secret burst into happiness deep inside her.

"There's something I'm good at, something I'm good at," the secret joy sang to itself.

Things got better and better, for not only did the rehearsals continue to go well and Ellen's finished scenery earn universal praise, but the floods came up on the marshes.

"Hurray! Hurray!" shouted Rob with delight as he and Rowena and William and Ellen, on returning one evening from Colonel Petrie's house, stopped for a moment in the churchyard and stared down on the huge expanse of steely water.

"And it's going to freeze tonight!" said Ellen joyfully. "Lambert said so. And he's always right."

"Two days . . . three days of frost," said William, "and . . ."

"We'll be skating!" finished Rowena, throwing her arms around Ellen in excitement.

To have acting and costumes and greasepaint and a real audience—*and* skating as well—all in the space of a few days, showed a bounteousness on the part of the Almighty that was without precedence in their lives.

"We'll have to look over our skates," said William, "and get the runners ground."

"Lord!" groaned Rob. "I bet I've grown out of my boots."

"Try them on tonight," suggested Ellen. "There's time to buy some more."

"Look! Look!" exclaimed Rowena, "It's freezing already." They all turned to her. Sure enough, her breath was pluming out of her mouth into the cold air in a smoky balloon.

"Look! And me, too," laughed Rob, puffing like a steam engine.

The dress rehearsal passed off with few of the mishaps that usually attend such occasions. Ellen shivered with cold under her cardboard Mock-Turtle shell; and Rob and Augustus, it is true, scowled murder at each other on the darkened stage; but when the curtain went up, there they were—two fat little men like eggcups—their arms entwined around each other's necks, grinning at the vacant chairs set out for the audience. Two or three of the field mice forgot their words.

"But that sort of thing does not matter at all," Colonel Petrie told William and Ellen while they were helping him to clear up. "The great thing about acting is to forget oneself. If one happens to forget one's words too, that is just bad luck."

"Felicia was wonderful, sir," said William. "She didn't forget a single thing."

It was true. Felicia *was* wonderful, for not only had she kept her head and remembered her lines, but she had also unconsciously *lived* her part. She was so exactly like Alice that she had had no need even to forget herself. Moreover, she had that happy presence on the stage which inspires everyone else to feel happy, too.

Not even her father could deny her gifts.

"Say it was a good piece of casting on your part, William," he laughed.

Ellen remembered the Colonel's remarks about acting the

next day as she stood in the wings waiting to go on the stage. Her teeth were chattering; she was cold and frightened; and her turtle shell had slipped askew.

"Forget yourself. Forget yourself," she muttered desperately under her breath. "Forget that Mother and Aunt Mary are sitting out in front."

Alice was talking to the Gryphon.

"It's almost your cue," whispered William.

"Fix it tighter," she hissed back.

"What?"

"My shell, of course. It's not straight."

And now she was on the stage. She was a turtle. A miserable, moaning, Mock Turtle. The tears were splashing down his cheeks.

"Sit down, both of you," said the Mock Turtle in a deep, hollow voice. *"And don't speak a word till I've finished my story."*

And now, in a lugubrious voice, he was telling Alice about the lessons that he learned at school.

"I only took the regular course," he moaned.

"What was that?" asked Alice.

"Reeling and Writhing to begin with."

Everyone laughed. They actually laughed! With a sigh of relief, Ellen plunged even deeper into Mock-Turtle-dom, and in so doing set one wave of laughter after another, rolling, splashing, cataracting across Montagu House drawing room. Thank heaven for Lewis Carroll! Every joke went home.

And now, soberly and sedately, the Mock Turtle was taking Alice by the hand and teaching her the Lobster Quadrille.

"You were wonderful," said William, smiling proudly at

her as she came off the stage. "I'd no idea you'd be so good."

Indeed, she had been something of a triumph. Aunt Mary said she had played her part splendidly; and even her mother conceded that she had been quite good.

She walked home up Northgate with Rowena in a daze of delight. Life was almost too good to be true.

"Ellen! Rowena!" shouted Rob, excitedly, as he ran through the dusk to catch up with them. "Have you heard?"

"Heard what?"

"The ice is strong enough to bear. Dr. Tuttle's been out skating all afternoon."

"Hurray!" exclaimed Rowena. "Tomorrow, we'll . . ."

"Not tomorrow," gasped Rob, having caught up. *"Tonight!* Colonel Petrie says the whole cast—everyone who can skate— meet him and Felicia down by the gate on the dam."

"Tonight?"

"There's a moon."

"Skating by moonlight!" sighed Ellen, feeling that she was about to melt away in pure bliss.

Then she came coldly to her senses and shook her head.

"I *know* Mother'll say no," she said hopelessly.

Yet, wonders of all wonders, when their mother was consulted she did not immediately refuse to let them go.

"Colonel Petrie?" she asked. "Colonel Petrie will be there?"

"Yes," gabbled Rob. "It was he who invited us."

"And Felicia is going, too," put in Ellen quickly.

"I've promised to teach her how to skate," said William. "Please, Mother, please allow us to go."

Their mother sat undecided and thoughtful for a full minute, trying to make up her mind—their fate dangling in her lap. Then she suddenly looked up at William and smiled.

"If Colonel Petrie has really asked you, of course you must go," she said. "But behave yourselves and be home before nine. And Robert, keep with the others. The ice may not be firm in the middle of the marsh. Do not go off on your own."

Rob promised.

Ellen never forgot that moonlight skating. And it was not just because of the dreadful alarm that followed, but because of the night itself. The cold froze her nose, sparkled in her hair, sang in her ears. It made sticks and grassy tussocks snap and crackle and the voices of the skaters ring. And the moonlight picked out the gnarled heads of the pollard willows and fell in white radiance on the acres of polished ice. But it was overhead that the true glory stretched, for a thousand stars, paled by the moon, shone down unwinking from the great arch of the night sky. She felt awed; solemn; and then, suddenly so wildly free and happy to be out skating in such a wonderful world that she sped away from the others, wishing to be on her own. She did an outside edge and then cut a figure of eight and then swept backwards in an enchanting moonlight waltz; for, though she was so clumsy in her mother's drawing room, she was as graceful as a bird on skates. Mr. Brooks had taken her out on the ice when she was seven years old and taught her to run, to glide, to dance, to fly.

"There, now, my little duckling," he had said at the end of the season. "You're already a swan."

Two years later when she had come upon Hans Andersen's *Fairy Stories,* she had thought: "How nice it was of Mr. Brooks not to have called me 'ugly.' "

William detached himself for a moment from the little spot of skaters circling around Felicia pushing her kitchen chair.

"Ellen," he shouted across the waste of empty ice. "Have you seen Rob?"

"No," she yelled back. "Hasn't he come down yet?"

For in the end, it was not Rob who had gone off and left William and herself, but the other way around. At the last moment, just as they were ready to set off from home, Rob had said:

"I've . . . I've lost something."

"Oh, goodness, Rob!" William had exclaimed irritably. "We're already late, and they'll all be waiting for us."

"You go on," he had said miserably. "You go on. I'll follow in a minute."

What on earth had he got up to? Ellen wondered as she turned to rejoin the chanting cast of *Alice in Wonderland* circling around Alice struggling to stand upright on the ice with the help of the chair.

"Will you walk a little faster? said a whiting to a snail," shouted Rowena.

"There's a porpoise close behind us, and he's treading on my tail," boomed the Colonel.

"See how eagerly the lobsters and the turtles all advance!" roared William.

"They are waiting on the shingle—will you come and join the dance?" sang out Ellen as she joined them all.

"Oh, I *do* wish I could!" said Felicia as the chair slipped away from her and she landed in a heap on the ice.

While they were all gliding, laughing, to pick her up, Rowena looked towards the dam and shouted:

"There's Rob."

"Where?"

"There. Sitting on the bank, lacing up his skating boots."

Ellen swooped away from them all and sped towards her brother.

"What on earth kept you so long?" she shouted at him.

"Doesn't matter. Doesn't matter now," he replied, hurling himself towards her, his skates ringing on the ice. "What are they all doing over there?"

"Felicia's fallen down," she laughed.

"What a night! What a wonderful night," he shouted in triumph as he flashed past her, his arms spread wide to the moon and stars.

And then it happened! The dreadful, unbelievable event! For hardly had Rob's paean risen higher than the willow trees than there was a flash—somewhere in Rushby—followed by the most appalling roar.

Rowena clapped her hands to her ears. Felicia fell down again on the ice. Rob stopped dead in his tracks.

"What was that?" gasped Ellen, in the silence that followed.

"An explosion!" barked the Colonel.

"In Rushby!" exclaimed William.

As they sat on the frozen bank of the dam feverishly trying to get themselves out of their skating boots, a plume of tawny smoke slowly curled into the night sky.

Ellen looked at it and felt her heart miss a beat.

"William," she whispered. "I think . . . it's . . . it's in the Market Place."

William glanced again at the dark outline of the Rushby roofs and nodded his head grimly.

"It . . . it couldn't be our house, could it?"

"No. Don't think so," he muttered.

As the skaters ran over the town bridge, the plume widened and grew much brighter.

Then two of the church bells began tolling—the tenor and the bass.

"It's a fire all right," shouted Rob in excitement. "They're calling out the fire engine."

The Colonel suddenly sprinted ahead of his erstwhile cast.

"William," he shouted as he passed him. "Keep the children together and away from the fire, till I've had time to see what the trouble is."

"Goodness! Your father can run!" panted Rowena admiringly to Felicia as he disappeared around the corner by Fen Lane.

Up Northgate they trooped.

"What's happened?" Rob asked old Mr. Wyatt, who had come to his front door.

"Don't know. There was that ole bang. . . ."

And now, they were panting up Saltgate Hill. Before them rose the church tower, strong and calm against an orange sky. They could hear people shouting and the noise of the pumps.

And then, suddenly, Colonel Petrie stood in front of them, barring the way.

"You are all to go straight to your own homes," he shouted over the roar. "That's an order."

"What's happened?" asked Ellen.

"Rowena," he continued. "The road is blocked along Ballygate, so go home with Felicia."

"Nothing's happened to Mother?" she asked in panic.

"No, child. No. Nobody has been hurt."

"Well, what *has happened,* sir?" asked Rob.

The Colonel fixed him with a piercing eye.

"It looks as though someone has tried to blow up Barclay's Bank."

When they got home, they found Florrie on her hands and knees in the drawing room sweeping up the glass from the shattered window and their mother sitting up in her straight-backed chair looking very white and shaken.

"Mother!" cried Ellen, running to her. "Are you all right?"

"Yes," she replied quietly. "Yes, Ellen. I am quite all right."

"What happened? What was it like?" burst out Rob.

As she looked at him, their mother suddenly swayed as though she were about to faint.

"Mother," said William, running to her aid. "You look ill. Are you sure you are not hurt?"

She shook her head.

"No," she sighed. "I just wish your father was at home."

"But it's all right, now," said William gently, trying to comfort her. "They've got the fire under control. There's no fear of it spreading."

"That's not what's wrong with the Missus," said a voice unexpectedly from the carpet.

The three of them stared down at Florrie.

"There's Constable Boggis waiting in the kitchen," she said grimly, "with Master Rob's Norfolk jacket over his arm. *That's* what's wrong!"

"My Norfolk jacket!" exclaimed Rob. "I lost it. Where did he find it?"

"Just outside the Bank," she said dramatically, getting to her feet and clattering out of the room.

"Rob!" gulped William, staring at his brother.

"Rob!" gasped Ellen. "And you said . . . you said . . ."

Then she clapped her hands over her mouth.

She could hear her father running up the stairs from the garden door. He was just outside; his hand was on the knob.

"*What* did Robert say?" demanded their mother.

Their father strode into the drawing room.

He looked quickly at the shattered window and then at their mother.

"No, Will. I am all right. I am quite all right. Ellen," she demanded again. "*What* did Robert say?"

Ellen, white in the face with misery, shook her head.

"But I *lost* my jacket," Rob cried out in anguish. "I lost it. I looked for it everywhere."

"What's all this about?" asked their father in bewilderment.

"I *lost* my jacket, Father," Rob tried to explain.

"Bother your jacket!" he exclaimed.

"But, Will," said their mother. "Constable Boggis has found the jacket. He found it just outside the Bank!"

"The *Bank?* How on earth did it get there?"

"I don't know. I don't know," shouted Rob in desperation. "I promise I don't know."

"Ellen," repeated her mother with mounting insistence. "What did Robert say. You must tell us."

Ellen looked helplessly at William and shook her head. William looked wretchedly at Rob and let out a long sigh.

"He lost his temper at one of the rehearsals, Father, and said something silly," he said.

"But I didn't mean it! You know I didn't mean it!" protested Rob.

"What did Robert say that he did not mean, William?" asked his father.

"Colonel Petrie said he'd have to embrace Augustus Peebles on the stage, and . . . and . . ."

"I didn't *mean* it!"

"And?" demanded his father. "Go on, William."

"I said I'd rather blow up a bank," burst out the unhappy Rob.

"You said *what?*"

Ellen saw that her mother had closed her eyes in horror.

"That . . . that . . . I'd . . . rather . . . blow up . . . a bank, Father," repeated the wretched boy.

"What an idiotic thing to say!"

"It . . . it just came out of my mouth."

Ellen had hardly expected the heavens to fall; her father was too controlled a man; besides, he had had eleven long years of coping with Rob. But she had not expected him to be caught up in a silent abstraction, either.

"Robert, what an *extraordinary* thing for you to have said," he murmured at last with a puzzled air.

Their mother opened her eyes again in surprise.

"Not at all, Will," she rapped out. "After all these bomb outrages, the neighborhood can talk of little else but of buildings being blown up."

"But, Cara," he replied, still puzzled. "That is not the same thing. Do you not see that 'buildings being blown up' and 'blowing up buildings' are two quite different ideas?"

What did her father mean, Ellen wondered.

"What is more," he continued uneasily. "It does not occur to anyone—even when he is in a temper—to threaten an act that it is quite impossible for him to carry out."

"I do not understand . . ." began their mother.

But William understood. Ellen saw that he understood. He was staring at Rob in alarm. A most unwelcome thought had clearly entered his head.

"You cannot threaten to blow up a bank, Cara, unless you have something to blow it up *with.*"

Ellen looked swiftly at Rob and gasped. The child was utterly dazed—and frightened, too.

"Robert, you have not been playing about with explosives?" asked his father.

Rob shook his head.

"No, Father," he muttered. "Not playing about."

"At school? In the laboratory?"

He shook his head again—almost absentmindedly. It was as though his mind were chasing after an incredible idea that had nothing to do with what his father was asking him.

Then suddenly, he turned around wildly and bolted out of the drawing room.

"I'll be back," he shouted as he thundered up the stairs. "I'll be back in a minute."

The four of them stared at one another in blank amazement.

"Where has he gone?" asked his mother.

Their father shook his head.

"I do not know, Cara," he replied. "But I am uneasy. Very uneasy."

"Rob couldn't have done it, Father," Ellen blurted out. "He was with us on the ice when it happened. Right down on the marsh."

"Was he with you all the time?"

Ellen suddenly felt sick.

"No," muttered William.

"Why not?" rasped his mother. "I told you to keep together."

William explained that just as they were leaving home Rob had said that he had lost something and that he would follow down later.

"What had he lost?"

"He didn't say."

"How long was he before he joined you?"

William stared miserably at the carpet.

"About half an hour."

They heard a door slam at the top of the house, and Rob clattering down two flights of stairs in panic haste.

He stood in the doorway, completely distraught.

"It's not there, Father," he gabbled. "It's not there. Someone's taken it!"

"Pull yourself together, child," said his father sharply. "What is 'it'?"

"The . . . the stick thing . . . I . . . picked up at East-wold . . . last summer."

"Rob!" exclaimed William, aghast.

"What does he mean?" asked his father.

"The engineers . . . they . . . they were blowing up the old breakwater," William stammered.

"And what did you pick up, Robert?"

"A short, fat kind of stick thing."

"Gelignite," groaned William.

"Heavens above!" exclaimed their father. "And what did you do with your stick of gelignite?"

"I put it in my museum."

"Your museum? Do you mean that attic next to Cook's bedroom?"

Rob nodded his head.

Their father sat down heavily in a chair.

"Good God!"

Ellen caught sight of her mother drooping sideways out of her chair.

"Father," she said, running over to her. "Mother's fainting."

"Put your head down, Cara. Right down. William, open the

window. That's better. That's better. The color's coming back."

"Yes," thought Ellen numbly as she fanned her mother's face. "It's enough to make anyone faint. We might all have been blown up months ago."

"And it's gone?" whipped out William, rounding on Rob. "You are sure that it has gone?"

Rob nodded his head vigorously.

"Sure. Quite sure. I turned everything upside down."

Their father shuddered.

Then, as though putting a nightmare behind him, he braced himself, got up from his chair, and walked slowly over to his son.

"Robert," he said quietly, putting a hand on each of his shoulders and looking gravely into his eyes. "Have I your solemn word that you had no hand in this affair?"

Rob returned his gaze, unflinching.

"I promise, Father," he replied earnestly. "I promise that I had nothing to do with it."

Everyone relaxed. For Ellen, the world had stopped standing on its head.

But the problem remained. There was the constable, waiting so patiently in the kitchen, to be answered.

"Now, let us be quite calm and methodical," began their father. "You say someone has taken the gelignite?"

Rob nodded.

"Who?"

"I don't know. I can't think who can have taken it."

"Who knows that you had it?"

Robert thought for a moment.

"Nobody in Rushby."

"You told your friends at St. Olaves?"

"One or two."

"Did you tell Augustus?"

"Of course not. He's not one of our set."

"Did you tell anyone in your set where you *kept* the gelignite?"

Rob thought hard.

"I might have told Dashwood Minor. He's got a museum himself."

"And did you tell him that your museum was in the attic?"

Rob thought for a little and then nodded.

"And are Dashwood Minor and Augustus good friends?"

"No, Father. You don't understand. The only friends Augustus has at school are the masters."

His father paused, considering this remarkable fact in silence.

"Still," he continued a moment later. "At least one boy at school actually *knew* that you had a stick of gelignite which you kept in your museum?"

Rob nodded.

"And nobody in Rushby knew that you even possessed it?"

"No."

"Sure?"

Rob was sure.

His father sighed. It seemed to all of them that they had come to a dead end. He sat down in his chair and cupped his head in his hands.

"Rob," asked Ellen timidly. "What was it that you had lost earlier in the evening?"

"My coat, of course."

"Where did you think it might be?"

"I didn't know," he replied.

"Think, child," broke in his mother sharply. "When did you last have your coat?"

Ellen frowned. It was the sort of silly question that always made her mad.

"If I could only remember," said Rob in anguish, "it wouldn't be lost."

"Calmly, calmly, Robert," said his father gently. "Tell us, instead, where you spent half an hour looking for it."

"In the lobby," he replied promptly. "Then in my bedroom; then in William's; then in Ellen's."

"Why were you in such a fuss about the coat?" asked William. "You often lose things and never seem to mind."

Rob looked uncomfortably at his mother.

"It was my new Norfolk jacket," he confessed. "I thought you'd be so cross."

"Robert," put in his father quickly. "When you found that it was not in the house what did you do then?"

"Why, I suddenly remembered . . . or thought I remembered . . . that I had left it at the Petries' after the play."

"And so what did you do?"

"I called in at Montagu House on the way down to the skating and asked Annie."

"Annie?"

"Colonel Petrie's parlormaid," explained his mother. "We can always check with her if Robert called."

"Don't you *believe* me?" he burst out, suddenly scarlet in the face.

"Of course, we do," said William.

"But it is a fact that we may have to prove in a court of law," explained his father grimly.

"A court of law?"

"We all think someone wanted to make it look as though you'd done it, Rob," said William.

"Me? But who'd ever do such a thing?" he asked in astonishment.

The answer seemed so obvious that no one thought to tell him.

"Cara, my dear," said his father after further thought. "Ring the bell for Florrie."

"Goodness! What does he want Florrie for?" Ellen wondered stupidly. "She's swept up all the glass."

When the house parlormaid arrived, he addressed her slowly and calmly.

"Florrie, I want you to think back very carefully over the last fortnight or so."

"Yes, sir."

"Has Mr. Peebles's son, Augustus, called at the house and asked for the children when the family was all out?"

Florrie looked laboriously back through the last two weeks and slowly shook her head.

"Thank you," he sighed as he told her she might go.

As she reached the door, however, she stopped.

"But he called for that box of pills for Mrs. Peebles, sir."

"Yes?"

"Go on," said their mother.

"Well, he came to the front door, ma'am . . . ten days back, it would have been, and asked for Mrs. Peebles's tablets."

"To the *front* door?" asked their mother.

"Why did he not go to the surgery?"

"That's what I asked. But he said he'd been told to call at the house."

"So what did you do?"

"Nipped across to the surgery, sir, and asked the dispenser. He hadn't even started packing them up."

"You left the boy in the hall?"

"That's right, sir. I hope I didn't do wrong."

"No, Florrie. You did what was natural. Now, go down to the kitchen and make Constable Boggis another pot of tea."

"Yes, sir."

When she had gone, Rob exploded.

"Not Augustus! I can't believe it."

"One more question," said his father, as he made for the front door. "William, was Augustus skating with the rest of you, tonight?"

"No."

"Well, that's that."

"Where are you going, Will?" called his wife, hurrying after him to the front doorstep.

"To talk with Mr. Peebles," came back his voice from the smoke-filled Market Place.

Natural Love
and Affection

❧ 1 ❦

It was on a late June day, during his first long vacation from
Cambridge, that William suddenly realized what he had let
himself in for.

"Goodness!" he wondered in panic. "How on earth did I
ever come to agree to such a thing?"

When he woke up that morning, he was still oblivious of
what he had done and was innocently happy in a sleepy sort
of way both with life and with himself. He looked at his watch.
It was twenty to eight—still ten minutes to go before Florrie
knocked on his door. So, turning over in bed, he drifted into a
pleasing reverie about Cambridge. The University had come as
a great surprise to him. It was so exciting and companionable.
The lectures and experiments had sent his mind darting into

all sorts of extraordinary places—places that he had hardly known existed before. Besides, there were the college debates and his friends' talk—and the fun. In short, everything about Cambridge made him feel warm and confident—as though he were a little drunk.

"That's it," he thought, grinning at the narrow bars of sunlight streaming through the slats in the blind. "I'm intellectually tipsy."

How else could he suppose that he—William Henchman—might perhaps be cleverer than either he or anyone else had ever thought he was? He had actually won a physiology prize. A proper University award. In his first year.

"Master William! Master William!" shouted Florrie as she knocked on the door. "The Doctor, he's out of the bathroom. And I've a-turned on the tap."

Florrie made this announcement with considerable pride—as well she might—for "bathroom" and "tap" were both novelties in the Henchman household. For Florrie herself, it was triumph. It was an end to carrying pails of water up three flights of stairs.

"Hurry you up, Master William," she bullied. "It'll be a-running all over in a jiff."

William shook off Cambridge and braced himself for total immersion in two feet of cold water. He shivered. It had to be done. One had to prove oneself a man. Today, just to show how serious he felt about it, he decided to count thirty, instead of twenty, before leaping out. Training one's mind was sheer bliss, he thought, as he slipped out of his pyjamas. Training one's body was a painful affair. Still, it had to be done. England and the Empire required it. Goodness only knew where he might not be wanted in two years' time. The Sudan? India? South Africa? The Suez Canal? In he plunged.

"Florrie says Father wants you," said Rob, bursting, tousle-headed, into the bathroom.

"In a hurry?" asked William, his teeth chattering as he rubbed himself vigorously with his towel.

"No. Just when you've had breakfast."

"That's good." His skin seemed to be taking even longer this morning to turn from blue to pink. "I've got my dumbbells to swing."

"Your silly dumbbells," muttered his younger brother as he flicked his face lightly with William's disappearing cold bath water.

"They're not silly! Ten swings night and morning, that's what Tindall of Trinity does. And he's stroke of the varsity eight."

"Well, you're *not* stroke and never will be. You don't even row."

William wanted to swish this impertinent thirteen-year-old sprat with the wet end of his towel; but he said instead:

"Rob, put in the plug and run a full cold bath and get *into* it. You're a disgrace to the family not bathing properly in the morning."

Coming down to the breakfast room, William saw at once that the usual battle was in progress between his mother and his sister. At least, it was not quite a battle, for Ellen was saying nothing. She must have laid down her weapons in defeat. She sat dumbly over her porridge, looking mulish and miserable.

"Really, Ellen," mocked their mother. "It's an absurd idea. It is not . . . not even . . . quite ladylike."

This was almost the worst condemnation that their mother could make. It was unanswerable.

"Now, if you had suggested that finishing school in Dresden, or . . . or bicycling over to Norwich twice a week to attend the

Ladies' Guild of Flower Painters . . . or even if you had wanted to follow Rowena to Geneva for that language course. But . . . but to want to be a *hospital nurse!*"

The breakfast cups tinkled to Mother's dangerously brittle laugh.

"Florence Nightingale was a nurse," muttered Ellen.

"But Ellen," ridiculed her mother. "You surely do not consider yourself a second Florence Nightingale?"

"Of course not," mumbled Ellen wretchedly, blushing crimson with embarrassment.

"Why can't Ellen be a nurse?" asked William, fresh from his dumbbells. He usually kept out of this warfare, but his sister looked so unhappy that he thought she needed support. "I think it's a sensible thing for her to want to do. And . . . and it doesn't matter if it's unladylike . . . because, because Ellen *is* a lady. . . . That's all that counts."

"You do not know anything about these things," whipped out their mother. "So please do not interfere."

Ellen suddenly burst into tears and fled from the room.

"There now!" she continued irritably. "Look what you have done! You do not understand girls at all, William. You have no idea what whimsical ideas they get into their heads when they are Ellen's age. Wanting to be a nurse, indeed! The whole thing is not only unfitting but also most socially unjust."

"Socially unjust? What do you mean?"

His mother had never bothered her head about social justice before.

"There are many poor girls in England, William, who *have* to earn their own living. If Ellen took a post as a nurse, she would be denying one of those poor girls her daily bread."

William looked at his mother narrowly.

He wondered if this were true.

"Now, eat your breakfast quickly. Your father wants to see you in the study."

This repeated summons "to see Father in the study" gave him a sharp twinge of anxiety. Now that the event was so soon to be upon him, his inside suddenly felt as though it were going to collapse. Then he smiled in self-mockery. He was nineteen—almost a grown man. And his father treated him as such. Besides, there had been no trouble between them since Aunt Mary's disastrous Zenana Mission Bazaar—and that was nearly three years ago. He had nothing to fear.

He found his father reading a large parchment document spread out over the study table.

"Ah, William," he said, looking up with a smile. "I discovered this old deed at the bottom of my security box last night and I thought that you might like to look at it with me."

"What is it, Father?"

"It is a deed of copartnership signed between my grandfather and my father in 1822. Sit down and read it. Some of it will interest you."

William sat down and studied the beautifully inscribed indenture made between William Henchman, surgeon and apothecary of Rushby in Suffolk, and Edmund Henchman, surgeon and apothecary of the same place, in which *the said William in consideration of the natural love and affection which he beareth for the said Edmund* agreed to take him into partnership.

As he read on, William began to smile.

"Look, Father," he laughed. "They agree to share the expenses of the apprentices, the horses, their stabling and food, and the drugs, phials, glass, fuel, and candles used in the business."

"Very proper. What is it that amuses you?"

"It all sounds so old-fashioned!"

His father considered the charge a moment.

"Times have changed, certainly," he said with a smile. "When we come to draw up *our* partnership, we shall have to leave out the apprentices."

William looked at his father's happy face and suddenly felt appalled. Stunned.

Join his father at Rushby? Lead his father's life?

"I am very proud of you, William," his father continued. "You will bring great credit to the firm."

William felt as though he had been standing in a pleasant meadow—and as though the ground had suddenly cracked open and swallowed half the world.

"Thank you, Father," he heard himself say.

Cambridge, physiology, Professor Tonkin's research class— they had all disappeared into the bowels of the earth. So had India and South Africa and the Sudan.

"We will have to change the candles to oil lamps," he joked miserably.

Inside, he felt stricken with loss. How could he ever have foreseen what Cambridge had revealed to him: the width and depth and excitement of the world? And the grief of it all was that it was his own fault. From his earliest childhood, it had been a settled thing that he, William, the eldest son, should study medicine and join his father in the family practice. Settled by whom? By himself—quite as much as by his parents. His future had been discussed over and over again— and he had not once gainsaid it.

"Can you spare a morning from your books to drive out with me? It's a fine day, at last. Not a cloud in the sky."

William looked at his father and felt more bitterly unhappy than ever, for his father's eyes were bright with affection.

He nodded his head.

He was trapped—utterly trapped—by love.

"Capital! Capital!" exclaimed his father. "Go and tell Lambert that we shall not want him. We will drive out together in the dogcart. I have poor Fanshawe to visit at Mettingham and a child with scarlet fever at All Saints Green."

William took the reins, spoke softly to old Pegasus, and away they went, the wheels of the dogcart bumping over the rough paving stones in the Market Square and then rumbling more smoothly as they entered Ballygate and drove towards the Bungay road. He glanced quickly at the river far below them on the right and at the wet marsh steaming in the morning sunshine.

Everything was a trap. Everything.

"You've not many calls to make," he said, tearing his eyes away from the scene he loved.

His father agreed. It was too late for winter ills, too early for accidents in the harvest fields.

"And last year's harvest babies have all been born."

"Harvest babies?"

His father laughed gently.

"But, of course. Did you not know?"

The nights at the end of August and the beginning of September were still warm—and the fields were bedded with corn stacks. What more could man want for the begetting of children?

William was both startled and amused: startled because his father had never talked to him like this before; and amused because, somehow, he kept forgetting that the older generation must know as much about sex as his own.

Then he felt grave again. His father would never have

spoken to him like this if he had not thought of him as a future colleague. His grief returned. He was trapped. It was monstrous that he was trapped. It was monstrous of his father not to have foreseen what Cambridge would do to a man.

As he waited outside Mr. Fanshawe's house, William stood at Pegasus's head and stroked him down the muzzle over and over again until the old horse rolled up his eyes and fell into a mindless reverie. On and on he stroked, trying to lull himself into the same acceptance of things, while the bees buzzed in the flower bed beside him and the vast silence of High Suffolk slowly crept upon his ears. Not a cow lowed; not a cock crew; not a single human sound came from the lane or the byre or, indeed, from the sunlit house into which his father had disappeared. The whole world—save himself—seemed caught in Pegasus's dream, basking in the heat after the weeks of rain.

In the bemusing, mid-morning stillness, he slowly forgot his own disappointment and came to think of his father instead. He thought of him driving, winter and summer, year in and year out, around this unheeding countryside—alone with his intelligence. His father was far cleverer than he. At the medical school at St. Bartholomew's Hospital he had won every gold medal of his year. And, besides, he was a naturalist—an entomologist—of international repute. Learned men were in correspondence with him from all over the world. Yet here in Suffolk he was alone. It came to him in a flash how desperately alone his father really was—and must always have been, for Dr. Tuttle was no partner of the mind; the old man was wedded to whist rather than to the practice. And their mother, he now saw, could never have been much of an intellectual companion to him. She had been educated to please; not to

think. And what good had he or Rob and Ellen ever been to him, he wondered sadly. They loved him—loved him dearly—from a distance, but he was forty years ahead of them down the road.

"Why did he do it?" William asked himself as he waved a fly away from Pegasus's eyes.

Why had his father condemned himself to Suffolk, to their mother, and to them? Was it because he in his turn had been trapped by *his* father? Trapped by the same affection? The same loyalty? The same queer, inbred bond between himself and the people of the remote farms?

William let out such a sigh that Pegasus rolled down his eyes again and blinked at him.

Then, on the instant, they were both of them wide awake.

The old horse pricked up his ears. And William pricked up his. A thudding of hoofs upon grass throbbed dully through the hot air. William looked across the deserted garden towards Mr. Fanshawe's pasture. The hoofs beat urgently like a drum tattoo. A rider was galloping towards them in headlong haste. As the heavy thudding grew louder, it seemed to shake the whole waiting world.

There he was, topping the rise—a farmhand up on a great Suffolk punch.

Seeing William waiting by the dogcart, the farmhand tugged at the mouth of the great beast, bumped to an awkward halt, and hollered:

"Is the doctor still at Mr. Fanshawe's?"

"Yes," William shouted back, feeling embarrassed and disturbed for some obscure reason. He hated shouting. It seemed a rude and startling thing to do in front of this great, silent, basking house. Someone ought to have thrown up one of the sash windows and answered for him.

The Suffolk punch clattered into the farm lane. William could see the rider's head bobbing above the top of the hedge.

"Where is he? Where's the doctor?" shouted the man as he turned into the drive.

"Still with Mr. Fanshawe."

"Tell him he's wanted quick, sir. Right quick. Up at Mr. Weston's."

William turned irresolutely towards the front door. One should never disturb a doctor with his patient. He wavered. But at that moment the great door opened. His father and Mrs. Fanshawe came out under the portico. He took her hand, smiling—murmuring some last piece of advice. Then he turned, and on went his broad-brimmed, old-fashioned hat.

"Father."

His father looked quickly from William to the farmhand still up on his huge mount.

"You're wanted quick up at Westons', sir," shouted the man. "Master's up on the roof."

"Up on the roof?"

"Took bad. Terrible bad. He's flaytergaistering the missus right out on her wits."

"Quick, William," said his father, leaping towards the dog-cart.

"Master's pullin' out the roof tiles and a-throwin' them down," shouted the man hoarsely as he wheeled the great beast around in the drive.

"Get ladders, man. We'll be with you as soon as we can."

"Mr. Weston?" exclaimed William in utter bewilderment, as they rattled out of Mettingham towards St. Felix Green. "Not the Mr. Weston who plays chess with you at the Rushby club?"

A gentler man one could hardly imagine.

His father nodded his head.

"Is . . . is he mad?"

His father smiled sadly.

"It sounds like it . . . at the moment."

"You mean he's been like this before?"

His father nodded his head.

William was appalled. The wild roses were out in the hedges flying past. The great elm trees at the corner stood heavy-leafed and calm. Everything was the same. Blue sky. Green fields. The flies buzzing around the horse manure in the road.

One could not begin to understand the injustice of life, his father said. He had known James Weston since they were both children; they had been to school together. He was kind, hard-working, and intelligent; he had everything to live for: a good wife, children, a prosperous farm, friends, his neighbors' respect. Yet he was cursed. Every three years or so he had an insane compulsion to kill himself. One day doctors might know more about the cause of these things, he said, and discover a cure.

"But this morning it is just a matter of ladders, William, and trying to persuade my poor friend down from his roof."

Mr. Weston was sitting astride his roof ridge, all right—but quietly now, leaning his back against the chimney stack, surveying his pastures in a dejected sort of dream, clad only in his nightshirt.

"Take your children home," said Dr. Henchman angrily to a knot of women gathered in the road, gaping at the figure on the roof. "Be gone. I am ashamed of you. A sick man is not a Punch and Judy Show."

As they drew up, William saw a middle-aged woman open the front door, recognize them, and then run towards them down the drive.

"William," said his father, leaping down from the dogcart. "Give the reins to that boy and come with me. I may need you."

They met Mrs. Weston some twenty yards from the gate.

"Doctor, Doctor, I'm so glad you have come."

His father took her hands, and the three of them stood looking up at the white-clad figure sitting so quietly on the red roof.

"I can't . . . I can't do anything . . . with him. I've begged . . . I've entreated him to come down."

"He is calmer now," he said gently. "So you must calm yourself, too, and tell me how this began."

"I should have known it . . ."—she wept quietly—"I should have known he was getting ill again."

Her husband had been anxious about the haymaking, she explained. Soon after they had cut the grass it had rained and rained. Ten days it had rained. And the grass was rotting where it lay.

"And yesterday, when it rained again," she said, "he stood at the parlor window and said the weather was a judgment on him. A man as wicked as he was had no call to be a farmer. His sins had found him out. The rain was a judgment."

She had been impatient with him at that, she confessed, with the tears running down her cheeks. He was a good man, she had told him a thousand times. A good husband. A good father. She had wearied herself out with telling him so. And yesterday, worried as much as her husband about the rotting hay, she had spoken sharply. Rain was just rain, she had said. It poured on Mr. Fanshawe over at Mettingham and Mr. Farrow across the Green. Did he think that they were wicked, too? And what about the people of Sodom and Gomorrah—where it never rained at all?

William had glanced shyly at Mrs. Weston on their first meeting and then turned quickly away, ashamed to be caught staring at tears on the face of a woman as old as his own mother. He riveted his attention, instead, on the figure riding the roof ridge. Mr. Weston seemed not to have noticed their arrival. Plucking nervously at the hem of his nightshirt and staring straight ahead of him, he was lost in his own troubled thoughts.

"Father, how did Mr. Weston get up on the roof?" he heard himself ask.

It was a fine old farm that had clearly come up in the world during the late eighteenth century, for a former owner had built on a third storey and given the whole a grand red-brick Georgian façade which rose sheer to a low parapet. Without a ladder, it was impossible for the distracted farmer to have scaled the front of his house. Yet this was what he had appeared to have done, for the farmhand who had brought them the message was now carrying a ladder across the farmyard towards them.

"From the attic," replied his wife. "There's a small dormer behind the parapet. I could not follow after him. He's locked the door."

"What was he doing in the attic?" his father asked.

Since it was raining again yesterday morning, she explained, and looked as though it were going to be wet all day, she had told him to settle down to one of his problems. It would take his mind off the hay.

"Problems?"

"Yes," she said. "Chess problems. In that book you gave him, doctor. They're a great help to him when he gets low."

"And did he do what you suggested?"

Mrs. Weston nodded grimly.

"All day and half the night. Locked himself up in that attic study of his till past three. Angry he was when I knocked on the door. Shouted he wouldn't go to bed till he'd solved the thing."

The farmhand had called a young lad from the stable to help him with the long rick ladder, and the two of them had now reached the front of the house and were slowly raising it to the parapet.

"And did he solve his problem in the end?"

Mrs. Weston could not take her eyes off her husband and the swaying ladder.

"No," she said abstractedly. "Tossed all night, muttering about somebody's gambit."

The arms of the ladder now protruded a foot or two above the top of the parapet.

"Father," said William urgently. "Mr. Weston's waking up."

In a matter of seconds the farmer came terrifyingly to life. He raised himself on the roof ridge as a horseman might raise himself in the stirrups and began feverishly to loosen a pantile beside him.

"Get away!" he bawled. "Get away, all of you!"

The farmhand and the stableboy fled as the heavy curved tile came crashing over the parapet.

"James," shouted Dr. Henchman. "James, stop doing that. I'm coming up to you."

"Keep away," bawled the farmer again. "I'll have none of you up on my roof."

But the doctor was already running towards the foot of the ladder.

"Father," shouted William, sprinting after him. "Wait. Let *me* go."

As they stood panting under cover of the front of the house, another pantile sailed over their heads and crashed on the drive behind them.

"Father, let *me* go. You're too . . ."

William could not say that his father was too old. Yet that was what he meant. He had just seen him run down the drive with the stiffness of an old man.

"No, William. He is my patient. My friend."

Halfway up the ladder, his father stopped and looked down.

"But stay there, son. I may need your help."

William watched him climb steadily on upwards and ached to see how stiffly and deliberately he placed his feet. His father was too old . . . too tired. No one had the right to ask such things of him.

"James, it is I—your old friend Will," he heard him say as he reached the top of the parapet.

A second later, a third tile missed him by inches. It came smashing down at William's feet.

"You're a fool, James," his father said sharply. "If it turns to rain again, you'll get the water into your house."

William looked up to see him swing one leg over the parapet. Now he had drawn up the other. He was out of sight. Leaning against the wall of the house, he listened breathlessly for sounds from above, his heart pounding with fear for his father's safety. He could not bear it. He could not bear to stand idly there below and not help him, and had just decided to disobey and follow him up the ladder, when his father leaned over the parapet and said:

"Go and fetch another ladder, William. God knows how he got up to the ridge pole. But I can't follow him without help. The roof is too steep."

William ran off on the instant around the side of the house and stumbled into the farmhand and the stableboy who were cowering from the rain of pantiles under the lee of the chimney stack.

"Another ladder. Quick."

"Another?" gaped the farmhand.

"So my father can climb up the roof."

The stableboy twisted around and raced off in the direction of the stack yard.

"That's it, Stan, fetch that little ole one lyin' along the fence," the farmhand shouted after him.

When it arrived, William saw that it was light enough for

him to manage himself—which was just as well. Not knowing how one should do these things, he placed it flat against the uprights of the tall ladder and edged it upwards as he mounted the rungs. As he rose up the side of the house with his burden, his father's voice came to him in a steady stream—clear, calm, and imperturbable. On and on he spoke, with hardly a pause. This was very strange, for ordinarily his father was the most silent of men. He was obviously describing something difficult to his patient astride the roof top.

"And now," his father was saying, as he rose to the height of the bedroom windows. "And now, after White castles then Black moves pawn to queen's third. It's the best thing he can do, I think, though Chamberstock had another solution, which was to move bishop to queen's knight's third and check. But it's dangerous, James. Very dangerous. It uncovers his own king."

William could see his father's head and shoulders now. They were turned towards the roof top. As the arms of the little ladder nosed over the parapet behind him, they made a soft scraping noise, and his father hearing it, without taking his eyes off his patient, reached back his hand until he touched them.

"A little higher, William," he whispered hoarsely. "But stay out of sight. You might startle him."

He pushed the light ladder up another two feet.

"Besides, there's no strength to the attack," continued his father evenly. "It's a mere feint. It's much better to move the pawn to queen's third as I suggest."

With the most unhurried of movements he turned back as he was speaking, grasped the light ladder firmly by the third rung, and hauled it smoothly up over the parapet and laid it flat up the slope of the roof.

"Then, he protects his knight as well as opening up a path for his rook."

"No, I don't follow, Will. You've got something wrong," barked Mr. Weston.

"Blind chess is always difficult to follow. It's easier with a board and the pieces. You'd see it then."

William waited pressed against the tall ladder. What did his father want him to do?

"Go down and keep out of sight," whispered his father without turning around. "And tell Mrs. Weston to do the same. Nothing must distract him."

"What are you going to do?" whispered William.

"Talk him back down into his attic."

As he climbed down, the stream of chess moves continued to purl effortlessly out of his father's mouth.

"Then White takes pawn with pawn and Black moves bishop to king's knight's fifth and—here's a good one, a brilliant stroke, James—White moves queen to queen's rook's fourth."

"Then what does Black do to counter that?" William heard Mr. Weston bark in a disbelieving yet interested tone of voice.

He heard no more, for he was down at the foot of the ladder by now on the quiet ground. Out of sight from above, he stood with his back to the house and stared for a moment at Mrs. Weston who was still standing in the open drive, watching intently every movement in the drama still being enacted on the roof. He saw her gaze lift upwards and knew that his father must be climbing up over the tiles. Then he remembered his instructions. He called her name softly, but she did not hear. He beckoned; he waved his arms. But she had no eyes for anything but her husband and his father on the roof. In desperation, he picked up a small stone from the gravel and threw it hard, so that it landed plump on the skirt of her dress.

Startled, she looked down at him.

"Father says we must keep out of sight," he said hoarsely. "He is going to persuade Mr. Weston to go down into the attic."

She understood. She nodded her head, and after a moment's thought walked quickly to a small rustic summerhouse on the far side of the lawn. It was a good choice. It had a small, diamond-paned window overlooking the house.

With Mrs. Weston out of sight, the silence of the countryside flooded into the empty garden. Not a breath of wind stirred. The lime trees in the hedge, the delphiniums in the border— everything—seemed caught in a glasslike trance. Time stood still. William stared across the green lawn, his mind in a turmoil yet his eyes active, noticing things that had nothing to do with his thoughts. There were still raindrops in some of the grass blades from last night's showers and they twinkled yellow and white and red in the sunlight. A cabbage-white butterfly flapped lazily over the pansy bed. Then, with his ears strained painfully for sounds that would tell him what was going on far above him on the roof, other small, quite irrelevant noises crept into his hearing. Pegasus was growing restive; he could hear him pawing his hoof in the mud of the lane outside and the soft jingling of his harness. Then a wood pigeon clattered noisily into the still air. The sharp rattle of its wings startled him and made him tremblingly aware of his own fear. The old nightmare was back. With nothing to do but stand and wait, he could not hope to beat off its terrible black wings. He hated madness. It terrified him. The madwoman in *Jane Eyre* had stood by his bed for years. He summoned up his reason and his manhood, and the terror slowly passed. Mr. Weston did not want to kill anyone but himself. He was not cunning or malicious—only desperate. Yet his father was up on the roof with him alone. Alone with a patient insanely intent upon taking his own life.

William stood by the ladder and stared somberly at the broken pantiles littered over the drive.

Five minutes, ten minutes, fifteen minutes, dragged on and on in the quiet garden. It was the longest and most anguished wait he had ever known. What could they both be doing up on the roof ridge?

The cabbage white was now flapping over the delphiniums. Pegasus was snickering to be off home. The farmhand was talking quietly to the stableboy around the side of the house. The world seemed to have forgotten the battle of wits taking place on the roof.

Then he was suddenly alert.

Mrs. Weston was pressing her face to the summerhouse window. A soft rain of dust poured down behind him from a crack in the parapet far above. Straining his ears, he could catch the faint tones of his father's voice calmly talking to Mr. Weston.

They were coming down.

"We're not through with it yet," said Mrs. Weston as she and William ran lightly up the stairs. "But thank God they're both off the roof."

They waited panting outside the locked attic door, getting back their breath and trying to guess what was going on inside. His father was still talking—still explaining. And, every now and then, Mr. Weston made a short, sharp reply.

Mrs. Weston looked questioningly at William and then raised her hand and knocked.

"Is that you, Mrs. Weston?" asked his father.

"Yes, Doctor. May I come in?"

"Just as soon as we have finished this problem, of course you can come in," said his father cheerfully. "In the meantime, Mrs. Weston, get James some breakfast and bring it up."

"Milly," rasped Mr. Weston in a harsh voice.

"Yes, James?"

"Bring Will a cup up too."

"Of course."

Mrs. Weston looked at William, and they both sighed with relief. Mr. Weston was not too deranged to have forgotten the office of a host.

Yet the next moment William was not so sure.

"Mrs. Weston," William's father had said. "Tell my son to bring up your husband's dressing gown. He is cold."

"I'm *not* cold," roared Mr. Weston. "Not cold at all. Take that back, Will. It's a lie."

His anger seemed out of all proportion to the cause.

"Nonsense, James," William heard his father reply mildly. "It's a physical fact that you are cold. You are shivering. Look, your hands are blue."

When William returned with the dressing gown, his father unlocked the door, and William, fearful of what he might see, looked over his shoulder—not at a lunatic but at a very tired, very sick-looking, very cold, middle-aged farmer, shivering in his nightshirt.

"Fetch my case from the dogcart," said his father in a low voice as he took the dressing gown. "And tell Mrs. Weston to pack her husband's valise. We are taking him to Mr. Haddon's nursing home at Bungay."

"Remind me, William," he said an hour later as they drove

home together along the floor of the Waveney Valley, "that I still have that child to visit at All Saints Green."

William glanced at his father. He looked tired, played out, ready for sleep.

"I'll drive you," he said. "I'd like to. We'll drive over this afternoon."

But he shook his head.

"You have had enough of the practice for one day," he smiled drowsily. "Lambert can take me."

William did not argue, for he saw that his father was already asleep, sitting bolt upright in the jogging dogcart, his old-fashioned hat sitting square on his dignified head. He smiled. It was always thus. His father was like Napoleon. He could make up for intense nervous strain or for a broken night's rest by dropping off during the day and then waking, so quickly and unobtrusively, that few but his family realized that he had napped.

Alone with the faithful Pegasus and the sodden marsh and the full dikes flashing in the sunlight, William gave himself up to his thoughts—if one could call them thoughts. They were sensations, rather: warm, deeply felt, all pervasive.

He was filled with pride and amazement in his quiet father. He saw him in a new light. It was as though in watching him run to the foot of Mr. Weston's ladder and mount its rungs so stiffly, he had had a sudden revelation of what his father's life in the depths of Suffolk really meant.

He gazed about him: to the far horizon; up at the arching, blue sky; across at the Friesian cows standing deep in the marsh, slowly swishing their tails against the summer flies.

"Drive me home by the low road," his father had said as they had set off from Bungay.

"It may well be flooded after so much rain."

"All the better," his father had smiled lazily.

All the better. All the better.

Flood. Marsh. Dikes. Fields. Farms. And Rushby. That was where they belonged. Both of them.

"About our deed of partnership," said the doctor briskly, suddenly wide awake.

William looked at him in astonishment. It was as though his father had seen inside his head.

"There's plenty of time."

"Time?"

"You remember the date on that deed?"

William was all at sea.

"Date? You mean when the thing was signed?"

"1822. My father must have been thirty-two at the time. After Waterloo—when Englishmen were able to travel again—he studied in Paris; then in Leyden; then back again at his hospital in London."

"Yes?"

"Well, I'd like you to do the same."

He had done well at Cambridge, he explained. He should go on and study further—beyond what was required of a general practitioner. Do some research. Go to Paris. Germany. Italy. See the world.

"And if you find the world a better place to work in than Rushby, then we need never sign the agreement. You are free."

"Do you mean that, Father?"

Of course, his father meant it. A man should not be bound by his forbears.

William felt a great gust of relief and affection blow through him.

And then, in the stillness that followed, he felt oddly sad. He suddenly remembered a kite he had once let go of as a child and watching it zigzagging high over the marshes at the mercy of every wind, mournfully trailing its string.

"I'll think about it, Father," he said soberly. "Truly, Father, I will."

Twenty minutes later, as the dogcart splashed through the puddles on Gillingham dam, Pegasus pricked up his old ears, whinnied loudly, and came to a terrified halt.

"What the devil!" exclaimed the doctor.

Approaching them from Rushby came a clattering cloud of flying mud.

"It's Lord Tarrington's Daimler!" exclaimed William in delight, as the hurtling horror passed them, showering them with dirt.

His father snorted in disgust.

"The thing's a disgrace to him," he said severely.

William laughed.

"You must not say that," he laughed. "We'll all be having them in time. You'll be driving around the practice, visiting your patients in one in a few years' time."

"In a horseless carriage?" expostulated the doctor. "*Never!*"

"A petroleum motorcar is its up-to-date name. And you'll see, it will be petrol and spare parts that we shall have to write into our deed of partnership. Not Pegasus and his fodder."

He was busy attending to the horse as he spoke. They were late for lunch. His mother hated anyone to be late.

Mud-splashed and weary, his father looked at him covertly— and smiled.

George

Ellen sat on her campstool under a cork tree and gazed westwards towards Cap St. Pierre and the blue waters of the Mediterranean sparkling in the early light, her lips smiling—and her mind and her heart smiling with them—as she drank in once again the color and warmth and the sweet smells of the South of France. Below her, the landscape lay clear-cut and perfectly composed, the blue sky arching high over ocher shore, dark sea, rugged headland, umbrella pines, white villa, and the rose-madder riot of the village roof tiles. It would make a splendid watercolor. Rowena would love it. But she must hurry. She knew that she must hurry, for in another hour the sun would blaze down with such white intensity that its heat would blur the shapes of things and drain the sky and sea and the

purple hill of their color. Besides, in another hour her father
would have finished his daily reading in Horace's *Odes* and
would want to set out for Bormes-les-Maures with his butterfly
net, and Rob, hungry after his morning swim, would come
running up the path from the pension, shouting that she had
forgotten to order their picnic lunch.

Languidly she squeezed out a blob from her tube of ultra-
marine.

Yet five minutes later she was still sitting idle, her palette and
paintbrush unused in her hands. She could not hurry. She was
drugged—overmastered—by the beauty about her. In the grow-

ing warmth, a cicada had begun ticking in the branches over her head; the smell of the wild lavender, which she had bruised as she had walked up the hill, hung heavy in the air. She sighed. It was too much—too sudden—after the cool Suffolk fields. And, what was more, it disturbed her. She felt strangely unsettled, for the warm wind fanning the nape of her neck made her feel sensuous and pagan—quite unlike her Rushby self.

"Ellen. Ellen!" Rob's voice floated up from below.

"Bother!" she exclaimed aloud in annoyance, for she had just pulled herself together, dipped her camel's-hair brush on to her palette, and astonished the blank whiteness of her sketching block with a triumphant sweep of blue paint. "He's much too early," she thought irritably. "He's not given me my full hour."

She continued her blue wash.

"What do you want?" she shouted down to him, without turning around.

"There's a letter."

"Who from?"

"Aunt Mary."

She glanced down at him inquiringly. Her brother was bounding up the steep path through the lavender, leaving great puffs of dust behind him. At eighteen, she thought, he was stocky and strong—and as tireless as ever. No wonder Professor Winthrop, the famous marine biologist, had decided to take such a dynamo with him on his Australian expedition!

"What's it say?" she asked absently.

"Don't know," he panted, throwing himself down at her feet. "It's for you."

How absurd he was, she thought, trying to hide a smile as she took the letter from him. Though they both dearly loved her, a letter from Aunt Mary hardly warranted such a breakneck climb in the heat . . . unless . . .

"Open it quickly," he demanded.

. . . unless one wanted news of . . .

"What's it say?" he barked hoarsely.

"Give me time," she laughed. "I can't tell you all in a second."

"Read it aloud."

"It may be private," she teased.

But the first sheet of the letter was not at all private. It merely told them the Rushby news. John Stacey had been invalided home from South Africa. Serious complications after enteric—poor boy. Mrs. Fisher had taken over the produce stall from his mother. And—talking about the bazaar—if they traveled home by Switzerland, please would Ellen remember to buy some of those wooden figures the peasants carved in the winter? They sold very well last time.

"Go on. Go on."

"Your dear mother is enjoying her Worthing visit," read Ellen aloud. "She writes that she and your Aunt Amy have driven twice into Brighton and shopped at Hanningtons and . . ."

"Oh, skip all that shopping stuff," interrupted Rob.

Ellen ran her eye quickly down both sides of the second sheet and saw at a glance that her aunt made no mention of Felicia Petrie.

"It's all right," she teased, looking down at her brother. "She's quite safe. She's neither eloped with Augustus nor announced her engagement with Mr. Brooks."

"Shut up," said Rob, going red in the face and seizing the letter out of Ellen's hand.

He read the rest of Aunt Mary's news impatiently and in

snatches: William was coming down from hospital for the sailing; the Archdeacon had preached well on Romish Fallacies.

"Give it back," demanded Ellen. "It's *my* letter."

"There's nothing more," he said, disappointed. "Except that you mustn't let Father go out in the sun without his panama hat. Oh, yes, and that you must remind him not to eat fried octopus; it does not agree with him."

Ellen reread the letter carefully.

"You've forgotten the postscript," she exclaimed. "Just listen to this:

" 'Tell your father that a young man called Dr. Hayward has taken lodgings with old Mrs. Wright in the Station Road. The Board of Guardians, it appears, has appointed him Medical Officer to their Poor-Law Institution. Dr. Tuttle says he knows nothing about the matter and is all at sea. Was your father consulted?' "

"Poor devil!" murmured Rob with only half his attention, for a brilliant gold grasshopper had landed on the back of his hand and he was studying it with interest.

"Why?"

"Why, what?" he asked, as the creature leaped off into the scrub.

"Why is Dr. Hayward a poor devil?"

"He'll always be hungry. Didn't you know Mrs. Wright never gives her lodgers enough to eat?"

No. She hadn't known.

Ellen went off into a dream, sitting there on her campstool under the cork oak, the sharp smell of juniper and rosemary coming to her from the *maquis* above, and the blue sea far below her slowly paling towards the horizon. The fishing fleet was returning to the village. She could even count the boats.

"Come on," Rob called out impatiently from halfway down the hill. "It's time we were off . . . and you've forgotten to order the cold *gigot*."

"Isn't it a strange sort of job for a young doctor to be doing?" she asked her father as they sat under an olive tree eating their picnic lunch.

"Why strange?"

"I mean looking after tramps and old people in the Workhouse?"

"Someone's got to do it," burst in Rob. "Why not him?"

"But what will he actually *do*?" she asked, puzzled.

"That's just it," her father replied gravely. "There's so much that needs doing, Ellen—and so little money to do it with."

He spoke of wards at Barton that were a hundred years out of date, of old men shut up in one wing and their old wives shut up in another, of the loneliness and dullness of the inmates' lives.

"Very like, the young man will soon be off elsewhere," he said sadly.

"Why?"

"Because he will have no power to put things right."

"I'm glad William won't have to do such a miserable job," blurted out Rob.

It was most likely Dr. Hayward's own fault, thought Ellen, dismissing the matter. He was probably one of those seedy failures whom William had told her about: wretched students who only just scraped through their exams at a third or fourth sitting.

Five weeks later—just home from France—she was sitting in

the window of the upstairs drawing room at Ballygate House, showing Rowena her holiday sketches, when a tremendous clatter—a fearful pooping and popping—began in the street below.

"Goodness!" she exclaimed, getting up to look out of the window. "What ever's that?"

Below them a man riding one of those new-fangled motor bicycles had come to a halt by the curb—a halt, but that was all—for the machine continued to spit and roar as though nothing would tame it.

"It's the new doctor for the Workhouse," laughed Rowena.

Ellen frowned. The seedy failure looked more like a space man out of a novel by Jules Verne or H. G. Wells than a doctor. He was dressed in a cloth helmet, a pair of goggles, long mackintosh leggings and a thick jacket, darkly spattered with oil.

"I don't think he knows how to stop it," grinned Rowena in delight.

But to prove her wrong, the machine at that moment hiccuped to a silence; and its rider, flinging his long leg gaily over its saddle, alighted, balanced it up on its iron support, and slowly began to peel off his armor.

"Don't make a sound," whispered Rowena in the sudden hush. "You'll see what he looks like in a minute."

Off came his gauntlets to reveal strong, thin hands. And then off came his goggles and his cloth helmet, and Ellen stared down on a head of thick, fairish hair. He was very tall—even taller than William. About six foot three. He stooped to pull off his mackintosh leggings, then piled them with the rest of his gear on the saddle of his motor bicycle, and then wiped the oil off his hands on a clean white cloth.

Ellen watched him with mounting perplexity, for without his ridiculous armor, the tall newcomer looked curiously vulnerable standing there in the middle of Rushby in his best London suit.

"He's not coming here, is he?" she asked sharply, seeing him turn towards the house.

Rowena shook her head. No, he was visiting Mrs. Jackson next door. Her arthritis was worse.

"But she's one of Dr. Tuttle's patients," she remarked in surprise.

"Yes, but Dr. Tuttle's gone off to Scotland. Couldn't wait till your father returned. He's left Dr. Hayward as his locum."

They turned back to the watercolors in Ellen's portfolio and looked at them in silence.

"What do you think of him?" asked Rowena, at last.

"*Think* of him?" Ellen replied crossly. "What am I supposed to think of him? I've only seen the top of his head."

Her crossness startled them both.

"Oh dear," sighed a crestfallen Rowena. "I was so sure you'd be excited at a new doctor coming to Rushby."

Excited she was not, she thought more calmly. But surprised and put out she certainly was, for whether seedy failure or cheerful success, a doctor ought to *look* his part. Ellen was a stickler for such things. If one was an old doctor, one ought to look like Father. If one was a young doctor, one ought to look like William. But Dr. Hayward with his sputtering motor bicycle and his goggles—and his indefinable air of high spirits —was not in the least like either of them. He was something startlingly new.

"He's a nine days' wonder," she said aloud. "You'll see, he'll be gone on the tenth."

"What do you mean?"

"You don't really think he'll want to spend the rest of his life looking after old people in a workhouse? It's a miserable job."

"Well, I suppose one's got to start somewhere," replied Rowena thoughtfully. "Even bishops start off as curates in the slums."

Ellen burst out laughing. The last person in the world Dr. Hayward made one think of was a bishop.

He looked even less like a bishop three nights later, sitting opposite Ellen on the other side of the dining-room table.

"Please invite him to dinner, Mother," William had urged when he came down from London for the weekend. "He trained at St. Peter's. And I'm longing to hear what he thinks of the great Sir John Grant and his researches."

So Dr. Hayward had been duly invited and had duly accepted the invitation. And here he was now, spearing unseeingly at his plate of boiled beef and carrots and talking spiritedly about the London stage.

"Irving, for example," he was saying. "You can have no idea of his quality till you've seen him. It's his presence. It's magnetic. And then, his voice . . . it's so passionate—so intense. He understands people so deeply . . . sees their tragedy. Why, his Shylock . . ."

She looked at him covertly through her eyelashes. He was certainly something new in Rushby; he was an enthusiast. And he had not the least idea that her father had never been to a play in his life, that William could think of nothing but his profession, and that her mother was only taking an interest in what he was saying because Sir Henry had happened to be knighted.

"And then his range . . ." he continued. "Hamlet, Dr. Primrose, Lear . . . Corporal Brewster . . ."

Looked at from ground level, she saw that Dr. Hayward had

a particularly frank and unsuspecting sort of face—and that he had a smudge of machine oil on the sleeve of his coat.

"You go to the theater often, it seems," said her mother, smiling.

Ellen flushed. The innocent remark meant a dozen dangerous things. Knowing her mother, she was sure that it did. It meant: "I think you are probably extravagant, Dr. Hayward, possibly frivolous, and certainly not as single-minded in your profession as either my husband or my son."

"I used to go just as often as I could, Mrs. Henchman," he replied ingenuously. "We were lucky at St. Peter's. The doorman at the Lyceum was one of our old patients—and he always kept a seat for me in the balcony. I used to race over from the hospital as the curtain was going up."

Her mother frowned. But at the mention of "St. Peter's," William suddenly woke up, seized the conversation by the tiller, and wrenched it on to another tack.

"When you were at St. Peter's," he burst in. "Did you ever work under Sir John?"

"I was his dresser for six months."

The two young doctors were off and away in the instant, the conversational bit between their teeth. Sir John's new theories about gastric juices . . . the new treatment . . . the new drugs. They were darting question and answer at each other with such obvious delight that neither knew that he was shoveling the apple tart into his mouth, unsugared and without any custard.

Ellen looked in her mother's direction and smiled. Their stagestruck guest knew quite as much about his profession as William.

But her mother had found new cause for frowning.

"Now, in the case of peptic ulcers . . ." William was saying.

"Peptic ulcers!" she exclaimed in shocked surprise. "Really, William! At dinner!"

"Discuss them later in the study," suggested his father mildly as he rose to leave the table. "I have a surgery at seven, Dr. Hayward, but I shall be back within the hour—when I trust that you will join me in smoking a cigar."

Coffee in the drawing room began in a stifled sort of hush, for her mother, clearly thinking that she had made enough effort for one evening, relapsed into a most formidable silence, and William—forbidden to discuss diseases—could not think of anything else to talk about. As for herself, she longed to ask the newcomer why he had come to Rushby. Did he not realize that down in the country he would never see a proper play from one year's end to the next? And why had he bought that awful motor bicycle? It was both noisy and impracticable. Did he know that it took him five whole minutes to get out of all his gear and wipe his hands clean? Five minutes each time he visited a patient! And it had not even saved him from an oil splash on his sleeve! But all these questions seemed too impertinent for so short an acquaintance.

In the event, it was Dr. Hayward who was the first to find something to say.

"And what about you, Miss Henchman?" he asked, taking his cup from Florrie's tray and seating himself beside her on the sofa.

"Me?" she frowned.

She hated questions about herself.

"Yes, how do you spend your time here in Rushby? What do you do?"

Do? What did any girl actually do?

"Well . . . nothing, really," she replied.

"Nonsense, Ellen," said her mother sharply. "She is a good daughter, Dr. Hayward. She helps me in the house."

That was the convenient lie. And Ellen—hitherto loyal to her mother in public—was suddenly sickened by its hypocrisy. For the truth was that her help was not needed. The house ran like clockwork. Cook cooked; Florrie swept; Fred polished the boots; Lambert dug the garden; her mother arranged the flowers. What was there left for a daughter to do?

"No, I do nothing, Dr. Hayward," she replied calmly.

She did not mean to flout her mother. It was just that, for some reason that was not clear to her, she wanted tonight to be truthful about the ridiculous life she led.

"She helps Nurse Hyde twice a week," said William quickly, trying to smooth things over.

Helping Nurse Hyde had been her father's idea. It was meant to comfort her for staying idle at home.

"I just hold the basin for her," she said.

"Well, that sounds useful," their guest replied, looking at her with a gleam of amusement.

"But it isn't really," she confessed candidly with an answering smile. "Nurse Hyde did quite as well before I came. She just put the basin down on a cottage table."

From a long way away, she heard her mother sigh with exasperation.

"Perhaps, Ellen dear, Dr. Hayward would like to see your sketches."

How oddly things turn out! In later years, Ellen was always overcome with amusement whenever she looked back on that evening. For her mother had been annoyed with her—deeply annoyed; and in her annoyance she had wanted her out of her sight. She had embarrassed her mother—diminished her, somehow—in front of this young man. She was sure of that. So the three of them had been packed off upstairs to view her watercolors which, framed by the enthusiastic Rob, were hanging in rows on the schoolroom walls. Their dismissal had been meant as a lesson, too. And a sharp one at that. For her mother had known very well how intensely she disliked showing off her work before strangers.

"Ellen's awful about her paintings," William told their guest as he lit the gas mantel. "She always points out the bits that are bad. So *I'll* take you around."

Then he turned to her.

"Sit down on the sofa and don't say a word," he commanded.

So she sat on the sofa and chewed her thumb, while the two of them stood in front of *Ellingham Lock* (July 1901). She watched them pass on slowly to *Maltings and Wherry* and then on to *Market Scene*.

"Bother the man," she thought in chagrin. He had not said a word. He did not like them. And he did not know what to say.

Then they turned to *Storm at Sea.*

"Where's that?" he shot at William.

"Walsingby. Eight miles away. Where we spend our holidays."

They studied *Sand Dunes in East Wind* and then came to a halt before *Eastwold Mere.*

Still he had said nothing. Not a word. She was maddened by his silence. People often made fools of themselves when they looked at pictures. And it had hurt her sometimes—but it had not been really important. But tonight. . . .

He turned slowly on his heel and faced her.

"What a joy for you!" he said quietly, smiling at her angry face. "What a joy that you can say it!"

"Say what?" asked the astonished William.

"Say what she loves and how *much* she loves it."

William looked from the pictures to Ellen and then back again at the pictures.

"Yes, they're jolly good," he said, scratching his head, still mystified. "I always thought they were."

Florrie, standing in the doorway, saved him from further perplexity. His father wanted him in the surgery, she said. Poor Mr. Baxter had thrown one of his fits.

"So many of us love things—love them deeply," Dr. Hayward went on, sitting down beside her. "But they're all bottled up inside us. We can't . . . we can't tell anyone about them. But you . . . with your wet gleams on mud . . . and your rotten stumps . . . and your rat holes in the bank . . ."

Ellen's heart glowed.

"And the way the wind blows the sand into ripples and curves . . ."

She was deeply moved.

"And puckers the water up into little shining plates . . ."

All her life she had been shouting down a long, empty tunnel. Tonight, a voice was shouting back.

"And the quiet mere . . . and the marsh bird . . ."

"Please . . . ," she murmured, happy but greatly embarrassed.

He glanced at her and smiled.

"All right. I'll stop. But you must show me some more."

She nodded gravely and went over to the cupboard where she

kept this year's portfolio, and they sat together with it opened out across their knees looking in silence at the Roucas fishermen mending their nets.

"You have no right to be so contemptuous of yourself," he said quietly.

"Am I?" she murmured without surprise. Looking again at her pictures of the South of France, everything that she had felt on the hill above the village six weeks ago was coming back to her: the warmth, the beauty, and the heady smells of lavender, rosemary, and sage.

"You know you are. And ashamed of the life you lead. There's no need."

"How do you know there's no need?" she murmured, slowly tearing herself away from the rich happiness of the Midi.

"Because you at least *love* things and can paint them. You have no need to be angry with yourself—nor, forgive me, with your mother, either."

This was such an amazingly frank remark that she felt a spurt of anger.

What did a man know of the inanities of girls' lives?

"Would *you* like to lead my life?" she asked with spirit.

"No," he replied, considering the matter. "But then, I'm a man. I have to earn a living."

One frank remark encouraged another.

"But why earn it here—in Rushby?" she asked.

"Why not? It seems a nice place."

"It's fearfully quiet. No theaters. No Irving."

"But it's got friendly people," he replied, smiling. "Besides, it has offered me a job. And I wanted a job desperately."

She looked at him inquiringly.

"Yes, Ellen, you've guessed it," he grinned back. "I haven't a bean."

It was not his poverty that puzzled her. It was the intelligence in his blue eyes, his warmth, his understanding. This man was not a fool. Not one of life's failures.

"But at Barton Workhouse?" she asked doubtfully.

"Oh, come!" he exclaimed, laughing at her expression. "It's not as bad as all that!"

Some of the tramps were merry rogues. They had sailed around the world—some of them; dug for gold in the Klondike; done all sorts of exciting things. No, it was not the tramps who saddened him. It was the old people shut up in those soul-destroying wards.

"Their lives are so *deprived*, Ellen. So lacking in pleasures. Anything the slightest bit new or different makes them quite excited. My motor bicycle, for example! I pushed it into the men's ward last week to show them how it worked."

"And did it?" she asked, her lips twitching.

"How on earth did you guess?" he exclaimed, laughing. "When I got it into the ward the confounded thing refused to go!"

"We're home, George," they could hear William calling as he ran up the stairs. "Father wants you to join us."

Then he burst through the door.

"Hallo, what's the joke?" he asked.

That was Saturday evening.

On Monday morning, Ellen rose at six, dressed herself in a fresh poplin blouse and a sensible skirt and hunted through her drawer for her starched apron and nursing cuffs, and—when all was found—brushed and pinned up her hair and surveyed herself in the mirror. Yes, she looked absurd! Utterly absurd! An idle young woman playing at nurse. Yet, this morning, she did not scowl at her reflection—as she usually did. She laughed instead. She felt too gay for a scowl. The sun was shining, and two thrushes were calling to each other across the garden.

"You'll need your bicycle this morning, Ellen," said Nurse Hyde briskly as she propped her own against the surgery wall and began packing the basket on the handlebars with an assortment of odd-shaped parcels.

"Why? Where are we going?"

"Bar of soap . . . scrub brush. Jeyes Fluid . . . Towels . . . Sheeting," counted the district nurse, feeling each parcel to identify it before stowing it away. "Here, Ellen, you take the bundle your Aunt Mary has packed up."

"Aunt Mary?" she asked in surprise, giving the soft parcel an inquisitive pinch. "What's inside?"

"Baby clothes," answered Nurse Hyde matter-of-factly as she heaved herself up on to her bicycle. "Meant for her Zenana Bazaar, I don't doubt. Not for this. Now, come along."

Ellen realized that the district nurse was playing her "secrets game" this morning. It was useless to ask her what this was all about. If she did, her old friend would purse up her lips and stay mum. Well, it hardly mattered! She would learn about it all in good time. So away she bowled behind her companion, past the Corn Exchange, down Blyburgate Hill, and now toss, bump over the level crossings, and out into the country. It was a glorious day. The sunlight fell, clear as glass, and there was no one about. So still was the morning, in fact, that she could hear Miss Hyde's button boots squeaking as she pushed down the pedals.

"And why are we taking this gear all the way out to Snottisham Common?" she asked Ellen roundly as they swept past Worlingham Hall.

"I don't know," she replied laughing. "I wish you'd tell me."

"Well, the girl hadn't got a thing ready. The caravan was quite bare. Not a cot. Not a blanket. Not even a shawl. Said she didn't know. Didn't *know!*"

"Good heavens!" exclaimed Ellen, and then wondered whether she had rightly understood what Nurse Hyde had just said.

"Silly young fools!" continued her companion with a hint of laughter in her voice. "To be married for a year and not to know what to expect!"

"But who on earth are they?" asked Ellen, completely bewildered.

"A young tinker and his wife. Babes in the wood, more like. A fine time we had with them yesterday morning, I can tell you."

"Who's 'we'?"

"Why, that new doctor who's come to the Workhouse—Dr. Hayward, isn't it?"

George Hayward! So that was why he had not been in church!

"Now that it's all over," concluded the district nurse with a grin, "I don't know which of the three to laugh at most."

"The *three* of them?" asked Ellen, her front wheel nearly wobbling into Nurse Hyde's. "You wanted to laugh at Dr. Hayward?"

"Well, I wish you'd seen him!" replied the nurse, laughing outright. "When the baby was born and wrapped in his father's shirt, off went the doctor on that motor bicycle—pell-mell for Rushby—and guess what he came back with half an hour later?"

Ellen shook her head.

"Mrs. Wright's bushel basket, her parlor cushion, and the green rep tablecloth snatched off the table."

Ellen laughed.

"There was nothing else he could do, he said, seeing it was Sunday and the draper's shut and Mrs. Wright sitting in chapel. But that's not the end. Guess what he'd brought them inside the basket?"

The nurse once again was overcome with laughter.

"A Sunday joint!" she burst out at last. "One of Wyatt's roasts all hot in its pan—potatoes, pudding, meat, and all, with another pan strapped over the top to keep it hot!"

"Good gracious!"

"They were in luck, I can tell you, that thriftless young couple of fools, to have happed on a doctor with a purse as wide as his heart!"

Ellen gasped. But his purse wasn't wide! He was as poor as a church mouse.

"Why on earth did he do such an extraordinary thing?"

"There wasn't a mortal thing to eat in that caravan, save tea and a loaf of bread—that's why!"

Ellen bicycled on ahead through Snottisham village. She wanted to think—and to keep her thoughts to herself. It wouldn't do. It just wouldn't do, she told herself firmly. Didn't he know that half the people in rural Suffolk hadn't enough to eat?

Nurse Hyde caught her up as they emerged on to the Common.

"If that silly young husband hasn't a bucket of water ready boiling for us, I'll brain him, Ellen. I really will."

The sunlight fell through the oak leaves, dappling everything about her.

"Odd sort of bath! And odder sort of bathroom!" thought Ellen as she smiled down happily at the baby in her hands, feebly splashing its limbs about in a copper preserving pan its father had just mended for a farmer's wife.

"Funny little devil, en't it?" commented the tinker, grinning down proudly at his son.

The little creature was wrinkled and old-looking—but certainly no worse than Etty's baby had been all those years ago.

"I think he's splendid, Mr. Hughes," she said. "You must be very proud of him."

She sat down on the grass, laid the baby across her aproned lap, and began patting him gently with the towel. This was quite the nicest job Nurse Hyde had ever given her to do. A lovely job. He'd be ready in a minute for Aunt Mary's Zenana Bazaar layette.

It was then that she heard the popping of the motor bicycle.

"That's him, Bess," shouted the tinker to his wife inside the caravan. "That's the doctor."

He was on them almost immediately with a roaring of engine and a flurry of flying grass.

"How's the family, Mr. Hughes?" he called out gaily, swinging his leg over the saddle and turning off the engine. "How's your wife?"

Ellen looked up from dressing the baby and watched him. He had clearly not seen her sitting there on the grass.

"Doing nicely, Doctor. The Nurse is with her now."

"That's good. Now take this," he said, handing the tinker a smallish wooden box before beginning the long business of divesting himself of his mackintosh armor.

"What is it, Doctor?"

"Kippers. Don't know how to cook them. But I expect your wife'll be able to tell you."

Ellen frowned. This was really *too* much.

Now he had taken off his leggings and was unbuttoning his jacket.

"Got any hot water, Mr. Hughes, for me to wash my hands?" he asked.

"Here it is," said Ellen.

He whirled around and saw her.

"Ellen!" he exclaimed in delight. "What a splendid place to meet you again."

Ellen smiled back. There could be no doubt of his pleasure.

"Tip the bath water out, Mr. Hughes," she said. "And give Dr. Hayward some fresh."

He stooped down beside her, the sunlight dappling him as he washed.

"I did so hope that we'd meet again soon," he said. "But I'd no idea that it would be here."

While he dried his hands, he gave the baby an expert look.

"Looks set for a long life," he remarked happily. "And less of a guy than he did yesterday morning in Mrs. Wright's tablecloth."

He rose quickly.

"I must go to his mother," he said. "Be here when I come back."

It was all too idyllic. The sunshine. The baby. The silly young parents. George Hayward. And Ellen went and spoiled it all! She shattered and smirched the idyll with her hateful common sense!

"She's going on quite well, Mr. Hughes," George told the tinker when he emerged at length from the dark caravan. "But you've got to feed her up. She's too thin."

The young husband nodded dully.

"I've got something in my saddlebag that will give you both a start."

And going to his motor bicycle, he returned with a bottle of invalid port.

"George!" exclaimed Ellen, outraged by such extravagance.

He was foolish. He was idiotic. He was making himself ridiculous. Joints of meat and kippers! And now port! It was out of all proportion to his duties in the case! She was so vexed with him that she put the baby back hurriedly in Mrs. Wright's bushel basket and stumped off across the Common in a rage.

"Ellen," he shouted, running to catch her up. "What's the matter?"

"You can't do it!" she turned on him angrily. "You can't. It's not right for you to try."

"Can't do what?" he asked, puzzled.

"It's not a doctor's job . . . " she began.

"What's not my job?"

"Giving them joints . . . and, and . . . kippers . . . and bottles of wine. They'll laugh at you. Then cheat you . . . then. . . ."

"Ellen," he interrupted her angrily. "The girl's *starving*. She can't have eaten properly for weeks."

"That's her husband's affair. Not yours."

"Ellen!" He sounded terribly shocked.

"But it *is* his affair," she whipped back at him. "And if he can't feed her then it's up to the Poor-Law Officer."

"That means the Workhouse."

"Well?"

"Ellen!" he cried. "They've just become a family. You can't mean that?"

"Yes, I do," she replied angrily. "If the young tinker can't give her enough to eat, what else is there to be done?"

"He did his best for her. That's why he went to prison."

"To prison!" she exclaimed. "Why, what did he do?"

"Went poaching and got caught. He's only just come out."

She glanced up at him, and her heart faltered. He looked dreadfully disappointed in her—contemptuous, even. She wanted to burst into tears.

"But . . . but . . . ," she stammered wretchedly. "You can't afford such things, George. You know you can't. And . . . and it isn't just this family. There's hundreds more in the villages—almost as poor."

"This girl is my patient," he said sternly. "The others aren't."

They turned and trailed back towards the caravan, their bright friendship much tarnished, and Ellen's new happiness torn to rags.

She was wretched. She lived through the scene again in bed that night and was overcome with despair. She hated herself.

"What did it matter to me what he did with his money?" she asked herself bitterly. It was no concern of hers. Yet dimly she knew the answer to that. That was not the crux. It was her brutal common sense that had been at fault:

"Rob always said I was too bossy," she thought as a tear rolled down to her pillow. "Well, he's right. Now I know he's right. And George will never forgive me."

He had left her that morning without another word, bidden Nurse Hyde and the tinker's family a cheerful good-bye, and roared away on his motor bicycle without once looking back.

She could not bear to remember the contempt in his eyes.

"He's ashamed of me," she wept. "He thinks I'm callous and cold. And that I don't understand."

In the morning, she awoke to a pale glimmer of hope. Surely

they would meet today, or tomorrow, or the next day? He would call to see her father, or they would meet at a party—or in the street? And then . . . they would talk. She would explain. She would put herself right with him.

But the meeting never came. Dr. Tuttle returned the next day from his holiday in Scotland and resumed the care of his Rushby patients; Nurse Hyde whisked her off to nurse some sick children in Norfolk. And all Ellen heard of George was the early-morning popping of his motor bicycle as he rode out to the Workhouse.

It was a bitter time. As the empty days and weeks slipped by, she felt shut up and sealed in a vacuum. William was away in London, and Rob was at Greenwich making his final preparations for Professor Winthrop's great expedition to the Barrier Reef. She longed to have them about her—to hear them just mention George's name. And the worst of it was that George himself was not in the least shut up. He was quietly taking Rushby by storm. She heard that Colonel Petrie had invited him to dinner, that he had gone sailing on the Waveney in the Pebbles' yacht, that he had given an exuberant address to the Working Men's Club. She knew, too, that he was helping her father at the hospital. Yet they never met. They never once met. It was so incredible that they never met that only one explanation seemed possible.

"He's purposely avoiding me," she told herself in despair.

Then came the bitterest day of all.

"I cannot think what they have been discussing," her mother said to her at tea. "That young Dr. Hayward has been in conference with your father in the study all afternoon."

"Has he gone?" she asked quickly.

Her mother nodded. She had asked the young man to tea, she said, but he could not stay.

He had actually been in the house and had gone away without seeing her!

She fled to the schoolroom and wept scalding tears—tears that the water colors hanging on the walls did nothing to allay. She stared at *Sand Dunes in East Wind* and wept afresh. He had understood so clearly that evening what had been precious to *her*. And, two days later, she had trampled crassly on what was precious to *him*.

August dragged by—and half September—and Ellen decided despondently that it was time that she looked again at Aunt Mary's notes to the Old Testament, for she had inherited, most unwillingly, from her aunt the task of coaching the pupil teachers at the Board School in their scripture syllabus. And the term was almost upon her.

"Goodness!" she thought on opening the notebook. "Who on earth wants to know about Jehoshaphat and Jehoram and Ahaziah's wicked reign?"

She sat at the schoolroom table and stared at the scholarly handwriting and wished that she were a saint like Aunt Mary or clever like William or just plain lucky like Rob. She was sick of herself, sick of the empty life she led, sick of Rushby.

As though to mock this gloom, a most cheerful noise suddenly broke out halfway up the stairs.

"Ellen! Ellen!" called Rowena excitedly, taking two steps at once up to the schoolroom. "Ellen, you'll never believe it!"

She stood in the doorway—her eyes bright as stars.

"The Tarringtons are giving a Victory Ball. Look, here's the invitation."

And she threw it down gaily on top of the Second Book of Kings.

"Bit late," Ellen replied dourly, reading the date.

The horrible South Africa War had come to an end nearly four months ago.

"Oh, don't be so cross," laughed Rowena. "Call it a Peace Ball, instead! Well, aren't you excited?"

"We haven't been asked to it yet."

"Don't be silly, you will be. The groom's driving the butler around town. He's got the invitations laid out flat in a rose basket."

It would be odd if the Tarringtons did not invite them, Ellen thought, for her father was their family physician. But then things were going so wrong just now . . .

"There!" exclaimed Rowena as the house shook to a resounding knock on the front door. "There's your invitation. I'm sure it is."

They ran to the window on the landing and peered down on a black-coated, black-hatted man, as grave as an undertaker, climbing into the back of a shooting brake, a rose basket held primly in his gloved right hand.

"That's the butler!" cried Rowena, clasping Ellen tight round the waist. "What are you going to wear?"

As the great night approached, Ellen realized that she had never felt less like a ball. Everyone was going to be there: Father, Mother, William, Rob, Rowena, the Peebles, the Petries, and the families for miles around that she had known and danced with all her life. But that was not the rub. It was George Hayward. He had been invited too. And the more she thought of it the less could she bear their meeting again on such a public and gala occasion.

"Well," she told herself, sighing resignedly. "He'll ask for one dance out of politeness—and that'll be that."

No one in the Henchman family was, in fact, looking forward to the ball very much. William hated parties. He always had. After he had danced one waltz, he would slip away to the billiard room and play billiards with himself. Ellen was sure he would. Rob, on the other hand, loved balls. But this year he was feverish about his voyage and about having to say good-bye to Felicia. And her mother—usually animated by such festivities—seemed oddly put out by the whole affair. As for her father . . . well . . . he was feeling old.

At breakfast on the morning of the ball, he suddenly opened his eyes and looked at Ellen—studied her as carefully as he studied his moths.

"My dear!" he exclaimed. "I had not noticed it . . . why, Ellen, you are quite grown-up!"

There was a note of sadness—almost of disappointment—in his voice.

"And I suppose that means," he smiled to himself wryly. "That means that *I* must have begun to grow old."

She felt pierced to the heart by his sudden awakening.

"Too old," he went on. "Too old to stand up tonight with my grown-up daughter."

"Of course, you aren't," she burst out, feeling tears in her eyes at someone else's grief.

"We have been invited to play whist, Will," her mother reminded him.

"Then, it must be the last dance, my dear," he said, smiling at Ellen. "But I think I'll leave the gallop to a younger man."

Yet for all this sadness now that she was actually at Tarrington and the ball was upon her, she could not help being swept up in its magic.

"You're shivering," said Felicia as they stood, side by side, tidying their hair in the mirror of the great bedchamber set aside for their use. "Do you feel quite well?"

"Just excited, I think," she replied nervously. "Aren't you?"

"Of course."

How could they fail to be excited? The four-mile drive in the fading light! The carriages, dozens of them, rolling up the long drive! The great house! The torches! The footmen in livery! The smell from the hothouse flowers as they hurried up the wide stairs!

"Listen!" exclaimed Charlotte Peebles. "The band's started up."

Rowena flung off her cloak, spread out her arms and swept into a waltz. "Ellen! Ellen!" she called out. "They're playing 'The Belle of New York.'"

And now, their introductions and curtsies to the Tarringtons duly performed, they were clustered just inside the door of the ballroom, taking their dance programmes from a great bronze tray.

"Gold for the ladies and silver for the gentlemen," laughed Rowena, twirling her card by its golden pencil cord.

"And look," said Felicia, reading the names of the dances. "There's a 'Two-Step and Cakewalk.' What ever is that?"

Ellen's eyes swept the long ballroom. He was in the far corner by the hothouse plants with all the other men. William

was introducing him to the Merriman brothers and now to
John Field.

"What's a cakewalk, Ellen?" asked Charlotte.

She shook her head. She did not know. She did not care.
She glanced at him again.

The band had just switched to playing the "Whistling
Polka," and a great wave of expectation seemed to sweep up
into the air, carrying with it the scent of roses and lilies and
orchids and the bitter sharpness of the french chalk. And in
that moment of swirling excitement, Ellen suddenly had the
oddest sensation of standing outside herself, hearing the girls
about her chattering like birds and seeing—as though from a
great way off—Augustus and the Merrimans and George and
her two brothers drifting slowly towards them.

"Ellen?" he asked. "Can you possibly spare me the first
dance?"

"Duty first," she thought in her detachment as they whirled
away from the others. Yes, he was certainly prompt in his
politeness.

Around and around they polkaed, the scraping of the fiddles
drowning their silence and Ellen, still quite blank of emotion,
smelling only the deep richness of the rose in his buttonhole.
"Much nicer than a carnation," drifted through her mind.
"Carnations are so . . ."

"Ellen," he burst out suddenly, "I can't talk with you . . .
I can't . . . while we're jogging about in this silly way."

"Duty and politeness indeed!" she thought with a mental
gasp, suddenly waking up.

"I can't, Ellen . . . and I've so much to say!"

They were standing now on a sort of small islet in the
middle of the potted plants.

"I'm so sorry. . . . Please forgive me."

"*Me? You?*" was all she could get out.

"I've been longing to tell you how sorry I was . . ."

"But . . . it was my fault," she stammered. "I should . . . should never have been so . . ."

"So right," he said quietly.

Right? She flushed. She hated being right. It was a horrible thing for a girl to be.

Then, looking up at him in her confusion, she suddenly saw the deep uncertainty in his eyes. She could not bear it. She could not bear him to feel ridiculous about the very quality that she loved him for.

"It was *you,* George . . . you who were right," she stumbled out. "It's . . . it's so much easier to be sensible . . . than kind."

He looked at her gravely for a moment, seeming to run over her features in search of a confirmation of what she had just said.

Then he smiled.

"Let's go back and dance," he said, sweeping her up off the islet of flowers.

"Yes, I've been so longing to talk with you about that morning," he told her, halfway through their second waltz. "But I couldn't. Something . . . something made it impossible."

Ellen was so dazzled by her happiness—so dazed even—had forgotten so completely the desert of wretchedness of the last few weeks that it never occurred to ask him what that something was.

"How are they both?" she asked him, instead.

"Who?"

"Mother and child."

"Mother fine," replied absently. "And the baby fat as butter."

The young tinker had got himself a proper job. They were over that hump.

Ellen's thoughts drifted away sideways like a sailboat that has lost the wind. Somehow, though she had brought the subject up, she couldn't be bothered to think any more about the tinker and his family. She and George had sailed past them a lifetime ago. They were no more interesting now than a blob on the horizon.

George's thoughts seemed to have drifted sideways, too.

"Ellen . . . please will you always say things straight out . . . as you did that morning?"

His words startled her out of her dream.

"But . . . but I'm so often wrong," she stammered. "And . . . I hurt people. And . . . and I hurt myself."

"I need it," he said simply. "It's a help."

On and on they danced, through the two-steps and the lancers and the cakewalk, and Ellen, seeing Rowena's face swinging by in the haze, wondered vaguely why it looked so startled and amused.

Out in the garden, standing by the lake, George turned to her.

"I need your help . . . always, Ellen," he said.

She nodded her head.

"And I need yours, George," she replied gravely.

During supper, he slipped the gold pencil cord from off her wrist and crumpled up her dance card and threw it away.

"But George, you can't do that!" she exclaimed, laughing.

"Why not?"

"I've promised two dances elsewhere."

"Who with?"

"Don't laugh. I've promised the one before the last to Rob."

"Your brother?"

"He's setting off for the Coral Reef on Wednesday. I shan't see him for two years."

Rob and Felicia circled past, joyfully clasped in each other's arms.

"If Rob can spare me a dance from Felicia," she said, smiling up at him, "I think I ought to spare him a dance from you."

"And the other?" he asked, answering her smile.

"Wait and see," she teased.

"And how am I to spend the last two dances?" he asked, amused.

Ellen looked swiftly along the row of chairs at the end of the ballroom and saw a sad young face.

"With Charlotte," she said promptly. "You must ask Charlotte to dance."

"That young man looked very happy dancing with Charlotte," said her mother to her father, when the five of them were driving home, tightly squashed, in the brougham.

"Which young man, my dear?"

"Why, Dr. Hayward, of course."

"So he should be, Cara. So he should."

"You mean . . . ," began her mother with interest.

"I mean, my dear, that we have just invited George Hayward to become a partner in the practice."

Ellen gave a gasp.

"Did you know that?" she shot at William in a whisper.

"Of course," he grinned back.

"But the young man has no *money*, Will," her mother was protesting.

Rob was making a faint sort of bursting noise—like the keg of homemade ginger beer just before the bung blew out.

"He can pay us back the principal in a matter of five years," her father was saying. "That's if he lives modestly—and does not choose a fool for a wife."

"When are you going to tell them?" Rob hissed in her ear.

"Sh! Don't be silly. It's not my job," she whispered back, smiling joyfully in the darkness at the happiness of life.

ABOUT THE AUTHOR

The distinguished novelist Hester Burton is known on both sides of the Atlantic for her rare ability to re-create the past in vivid and memorable terms. She won the Carnegie Medal in England for *Time of Trial; Beyond the Weir Bridge* was chosen as a Notable Book of 1970 by the American Library Association; and she has received many other honors and awards for her writing. The six episodes that make up THE HENCHMANS AT HOME are based on research and actual reminiscences of local people, as well as on Mrs. Burton's deep familiarity with rural Suffolk. Readers who enjoyed her earlier book *Castors Away!* will recognize the Henchmans as descendants of the Tom Henchman who fought at Trafalgar and later studied medicine. Thus, there is a continuity backwards and forwards in history in Hester Burton's novels. An Oxford graduate herself, Mrs. Burton is married to an Oxford don, a classicist who shares her interest in history. The Burtons live in Kidlington, England.

ABOUT THE ILLUSTRATOR

Victor G. Ambrus lives in Hampshire, England, and knows well the Suffolk countryside where much of the action in THE HENCHMANS AT HOME takes place.

Born in Budapest, Victor Ambrus attended the Hungarian Academy of Fine Art. He left Hungary after the 1956 uprisings and continued his studies at the Royal College of Art in London. Although principally a free-lance illustrator, Mr. Ambrus also lectures at the Guildford School of Art in Surrey. He has illustrated many children's books, and in 1965 received the British Library Association's Kate Greenaway Medal for that year's most outstanding illustrated book for children.